THE FATE OF
MARY ROSE

THE FATE OF MARY ROSE

Caroline Blackwood

JONATHAN CAPE
THIRTY BEDFORD SQUARE LONDON

First published 1981
Copyright © 1981 by Caroline Blackwood
Jonathan Cape Ltd, 30 Bedford Square, London WC1

British Library Cataloguing in Publication Data

Blackwood, Caroline
The fate of Mary Rose.
I. Title
823'.9'1F   PR6052.L3423F/

ISBN 0–224–01791–8

Phototypeset by
Western Printing Services Ltd, Bristol
and printed in Great Britain by
St. Edmundsbury Press, Suffolk

To Evgenia, Ivana and Sheridan

Chapter One

She was dead even before I became aware of her existence. When I first heard the news that she was missing it interested me very little. I never for a moment guessed how soon she'd seem to become a part of my household — that often I'd start to think that she was more my own child than the sickly little skinny Mary Rose. How could I have known that I'd shortly get the eerie feeling that this unfortunate small girl had come out of her grave in order to sit on the sofa in my Tudor cottage — a ghostly presence that listened with avid interest to the gruesome details of her own fate as they were broadcast hourly on the radio?

But if in the end she was to seem to be more my child than my own child . . . she was really the child of the media. She emerged from the glass of the television set in my living room.

She looked deceptively innocent in the photograph that had been given out to the police by her mother. She had a grin with a big gap where her front tooth was missing. She had freckles and fat pigtails which gave a pleasantly old-fashioned flavour to her appearance. Her commonplace cheery little face gave no hint of the degree to which later she was to tyrannise me. 'Damn her!' I was to shout and later I felt disgusted by the callousness of such a curse. 'Damn that little dead Maureen!'

My wife was ironing sheets when she heard that six-year-old Maureen Sutton was missing from her home in Kent. I had long ago given up trying to persuade Cressida to send all the household sheets and towels to the laundry – just as I had long ago stopped suggesting that she employ a girl from the village to help her to take care of Mary Rose. An odd persecuted expression came into Cressida's eyes whenever I made any such suggestion. She seemed insulted and wounded as if I had unjustly accused her of some criminal inadequacy. My wife had very beautiful eyes. They were aquamarine and when she was upset or frightened her pupils shrunk until they looked like those of an angry parrot. At times they seemed to vanish. Then she had the stare both blind and perversely penetrating of the blank eyes of ancient statues.

'Oh, my God! That's a local child that's missing!' Cressida was standing staring at the television. For a moment she stopped her compulsive ironing. A warm singeing smell rose from the great white soggy sheet that was draped over her ironing board.

'What local child is missing?' I asked. I had just watched President Carter announcing his newest plans for a settlement in the Middle East. I felt I could see the bright gleam of his idiocy reflected in every single one of his terrible tomb-like teeth. I had watched thousands of Italians milling outside St Peter's as they mourned their recently appointed Pope. The camera showed a close-up of two black-veiled women. They were sobbing. I felt disgusted and bored with world news on television and I started to flick restlessly through the headlines in the newspaper. 'T.U.C. and Government fail to agree on pay curb formula.' I helped myself to a large glass of whisky. It was only six o'clock but I was already exhausted. I was suffering from a horrible hangover, for I had been excessively drunk the evening before. I had gone out to the village pub and left Cressida as usual ironing her hand-washed sheets. All the double whiskies I had drunk in the Red Lion were giving me an unpleasant prickling sensation all over my skin. It was as if every pore was erupting with alcohol. I felt poisoned. Bloody hell! Bloody hell! I drank more whisky, hoping it might kill the feeling that I

8

was killing myself.

I always got drunk when I came down to Kent to visit my wife in her cottage. At the beginning of our marriage I drove down to see her about once a month. After that I came much less.

I hated visiting her. We were much too polite to each other when I came to stay. Our unflagging courtesy was like a cord that bound us together and also choked us. The consideration and solicitude we showed for each other made us seem a model couple. If we had been photographed together we might have looked enviable. Both of us in our early thirties. Cressida, so delicate and blonde. Myself, Rowan Anderson, the devoted husband, dark and tall, a man of obvious elegance and education. Oh, we could have looked an ideally well-matched couple in some photograph! And when we were together all I wanted to do was drink. I loathed the way we had learned to skate so gracefully on the ice of our own politeness.

Whenever I telephoned Cressida to say I was coming down to see her, she sounded pleased. But only a little pleased. She asked what I would like for my dinner. If I chose fish, she went off to the fishmonger and bought some. She invariably prepared it very nicely with a delicate sauce. She was a good cook. She baked all her own bread. She made all her own jam. She did everything to save me money.

When I arrived in the evening she always had a cheerful log fire blazing for me in the living room. She put out a bottle of whisky beside my favourite chair. There would be flowers in the vase beside my bed. She remembered the names of the wines I liked and at dinner they were faithfully produced for me.

I ate alone when I visited my wife. She served me my food on a little bamboo table in front of the television. Cressida herself never seemed to be hungry. She ate a sandwich, she nibbled at a biscuit but she never sat down to regular meals. Cressida made herself very busy while I was eating my dinner. Eight o'clock was the child's bed-

9

time. It was then that my wife started bathing Mary Rose and shampooing her hair. She cleaned the child's teeth, and she read her bedtime stories and she listened to her prayers. But Cressida was also extremely attentive to my needs if ever I had any. I could never feel neglected. If I asked for salt or pepper or lemon or some such thing she scurried off to the kitchen to get it for me. The way she ran so obediently to get whatever I asked for reminded me of a little girl.

Whatever my wife cooked for me I praised excessively, but I drank so much whisky that it killed my appetite. Once she went upstairs to read stories to Mary Rose in her bedroom, I often tiptoed to the lavatory with my plate and flushed down every scrap of food that she had painstakingly prepared for me.

At some point during my visit I always said how glad I was to be in the cottage. I also said how pleasant and cosy she had made it. I could be extremely appreciative and pleasant when I chose. I don't think my wife ever realised how much I hated the nasty little house she had made me buy for her in Beckham. Her cottage always gave me a feeling of violent claustrophobia. I found it utterly repulsive, it was so poky and quaint. Although it was a genuine period house it reminded me of the worst kind of bogus ye olde worlde tea shops that cater for foreign tourists.

I always told my wife that I found it extremely comfortable. In fact I found it the reverse. It had an interior so dark one often had to switch on a light in order to read in the daytime. The windows of the cottage were tiny and latticed and the glass was opaque in their minute diamond panes. I am very tall and I constantly cracked my head on its absurdly low doorways and its fusty old painted beams. The staircase that led to the bedrooms was so narrow, rickety, and steep it was more like a ladder than a proper staircase. The floor in the living room was badly warped and the way that it sloped made me feel seasick. Still I was careful never to let my wife know how detestable I found her cottage. It was her dream house. I therefore felt a little polite hypocrisy was preferable to causing her pain.

I was equally dishonest about my attitude to Mary Rose. I repeatedly asked Cressida how the child was doing at school and from my earnest and concerned tones no one could have realised how little it interested me.

I never forgot to bring Mary Rose some awful plastic toy when I came down from London. When I arrived I always gave the child a hearty kiss and a hug. I sometimes took her out for short walks. She seemed to regard me with mistrust and I never felt she enjoyed these uninspiring little expeditions. She gave me the impression she would have much preferred to stay at home with her mother. In the evenings I became an over-merry and raucous father when I gave her a ride up to bed on my back.

I invariably told Cressida that I thought it was marvellous how well Mary Rose was looking. I said it was a credit to her. Strangely enough, Mary Rose never looked particularly well. Although I have never seen a child that received more care and attention from its mother, Mary Rose always looked anxious and depressed. Cressida's entire life revolved round the upbringing of Mary Rose. She seemed to regard it as her sacred mission. Her days were spent cooking, ironing, sewing, washing, for Mary Rose. Cressida worried about the child's manners, and she worried about her schooling. Although my wife spent hours with her every evening going through her homework, Mary Rose was rather backward. Cressida scolded the child and she praised her extravagantly. She slapped her and she kissed her and she weighed her every week. Although Cressida never read very much, she bought herself books on child development and psychology. I found my wife's interests tedious in the extreme. That of course I was much too polite to say.

Mary Rose was unlucky. She did not inherit her mother's beauty. Cressida was brilliantly fair and I am very dark. Our daughter had unmemorable colouring. Her hair was a drab grey-brown – the colour of a mouse.

11

Although Cressida was fanatical in her insistence that Mary Rose be provided with the most perfectly balanced diet – although my wife took the child for regular medical check-ups and made her walk for an hour in the fresh air every afternoon although she seemed always to be stuffing Mary Rose with iron and vitamins, with cod liver oil, wheat germ and yeast and various other nutritional supplements – Mary Rose still looked quite ill. Her face was small and pinched and she had irregular features. Her arms and legs were like small white sticks. She had a chest that was puny and ill-developed. Under her eyes there were faint mauve patches of tension.

Mary Rose always looked very clean because my wife made her wash so often. 'Don't forget your ears, dearest!' 'Don't forget your teeth!' 'Don't forget your hands!' 'Don't forget your neck!' I used to hear Cressida issuing her orders and I shivered. They made me feel I was back at my hated boarding school.

I tried my best to feel a little affection for Mary Rose, but I found it difficult. She was such a dim, timid child and she seemed to have so little personality. She was extremely well behaved but I couldn't find her interesting and it was so hard to make her smile.

'Oh, my God!' Cressida said. 'That child is missing from Fulton Road. I know Fulton Road. It's quite near here. It's up in the council estate!'

I noticed Cressida was staring at the television with an oddly demented expression in her aquamarine eyes and she was holding up her steam-iron as if it was a shield with which she was trying to protect her breasts. I looked up at the television screen in bemused silence. Little Maureen Sutton had entered our cottage and I was too preoccupied with my own dissatisfaction to register the importance of her arrival. I saw the flash of a child's happy face. Then the image vanished and was replaced by a shot of a football match.

I helped myself to a stiff whisky. If Cressida, who drank nothing herself, hated me drinking so much she never tried to stop me. It was the unwritten law of our relationship that I must do exactly as I wished.

'The council estate,' I said to my wife. I became slow-witted when I visited Cressida's cottage. I felt my mind was stagnating largely because I lacked all function from the moment I entered my wife's household. Cressida kept herself tirelessly busy from morning till night and the sight of her doing so much work made me feel demoralised.

Although I always politely offered to help when I saw Cressida down on her knees scrubbing the kitchen floor or when she came staggering back from the woodshed carrying a heavy basket of logs, she immediately refused and made me feel it would be impolite to insist.

Staying in her cottage I felt like a disgusting lounge lizard – a horrible male chauvinist pig who soaked on whisky while his wife devoted every waking second to attending to his crass and selfish needs. When I saw the tears streaming down Cressida's cheeks as she peeled the onions for some elaborate and totally undesired dish she was preparing for my dinner, I longed to be back in my flat in London where I cooked for myself or went out to restaurants.

I have always wanted my life to be as simple as possible. I am a successful historian. I am both ambitious and hardworking. I became idle and functionless when I visited my wife but when I was in London I was immensely disciplined. Every moment that I was not working I saw as wasted. Gloria, who had been my mistress for several years, often complained I had only ever been in love with my work. She saw this as a weakness. I saw it as a strength.

It was partly because I resented being separated from my books and my papers that I found the rare visits I made to see my wife so painful. I never brought any of my work with me when I came down to the cottage. I knew it would be impossible for me to concentrate on anything more intellectually taxing than newspaper headlines in

13

the atmosphere Cressida created. There was only one tiny pine bookshelf in her cottage. She had put it up herself, using some kind of do-it-yourself tool kit. It contained only books on child care and jam and cake-making. It had magazines full of crochet and knitting patterns. I praised the money-saving skill with which Cressida had erected this shelf yet the sight of its contents gave me a feeling of despondency and paralysis. The life she had chosen because she saw it as pure and idyllic to me seemed stultifyingly pointless. I never understood how Cressida managed to endure the monotony of her housebound existence. She knew very well that I was both willing and financially able to help her to do something more rewarding with her life than building do-it-yourself shelves, boiling carrots and brussels sprouts, rubbing polish on Mary Rose's indoor shoes.

Cressida had not been well educated. I wished she would go back to school. I longed for her to say that she wanted to study something, but she seemed to have no intellectual curiosity. When I saw the way the skin on her hands had become scarlet and flaky because she spent so much time hand-scrubbing our sheets and towels I felt only exasperation and contempt for her. When I looked at my wife's ruined hands they made me feel slightly sick.

The evening Cressida told me that Maureen Sutton was missing from her home in our local council estate my response was only my usual irrational gratitude that the council estate existed. My wife so deplored and resented the fact that this sprawling conglomeration of uniformly ugly buildings had been erected three years before on the fringe of her beloved and picturesque Beckham that I took a maliciously perverse pleasure in its proximity.

I had always disliked Beckham. Every cobble in its narrow and ancient streets looked as if it had been polished by hand. I felt it was both too near London and at the same time too far from any city. It seemed to me a place where all the odious gentility of suburbia had made some kind of arid and indolent marriage with the sleepy

14

desolation of the forgotten agricultural hamlet.

All the fronts of Beckham's tiny shops were freshly painted and snowy white. Beckham had rows of perfect little salmon pink period houses which faced a village green so well-mown and emerald-smooth all it lacked was a maypole. To the left of the green there was the plump and bun-like form of Beckham's showpiece oast-house which now had little function except to provide obligatory Kentish colour. It had been converted into a luxurious studio which was inhabited by a couple of elderly and rather bun-like homosexuals who loved French cooking and spent a lot of their time doing atrocious watercolours of the village.

I found Beckham suffocating in the summer when it was at its prettiest and all the gardens of its bijou houses were a blaze of colour like the illustrations in a bulb catalogue. One heard the hypnotic humming of bees as they swarmed in the great clusters of wistaria and honeysuckle that obscured so many of the mullioned windows of Beckham's Elizabethan cottages. One heard the soft clop of balls as decrepit old men wearing white flannels turned back into young boys as they played cricket on the green.

'Isn't it peaceful?' my wife would say to me.

'It certainly is . . .'

Although I detested Beckham in the summer I found it even more depressing in the winter when the spire of its toy-like church looked as if it had been blocked out in black ink against a sky doomed to remain an unchanging desolate grey – when every tree appeared to be suffering from some fearful disease that had reduced it to a sad dark silhouette of tangled invalid sticks. When I stayed with Cressida in January I always felt it was utterly inconceivable that spring could ever come again.

In winter the whole village often appeared to be totally deserted. Once the commuters had left for London the women with babies and the old people stayed indoors where, as far as I could see, they passed their days in much

15

the same way as my wife. They washed their clothes and their dishes. They did ironing, they cooked and they polished their furniture. They fed their dogs and they pottered about their houses and they watched their televisions which had aerials they had tried their best to hide by placing them behind the stacks of their period chimneys.

'I love the quiet,' Cressida would say. And certainly Beckham in the winter was very quiet indeed. Occasionally the silence was broken by the sound of a van as it went rattling through the empty streets bringing in milk and eggs and vegetables from the neighbouring farms. Sometimes one heard the noise of the doctor's car as he went out on a call. Every half hour, monotonously, there was the hoot and the rattle of the passing London train. But quite often there was nothing but the sound of rain and wind.

At half past three every weekday Beckham came alive for a few minutes when the school released its pupils. Boys and girls wearing maroon blazers and gymslips giggled and shouted as they raced back to their homes. Then Beckham once again became silent as its older children started watching television.

I have never liked drinking in pubs but when I stayed with my wife in Beckham I always went out in the evenings and drank alone in the Red Lion. I found it such a strain to sit and watch television while Cressida did housework far into the night. Once Mary Rose had gone to sleep Cressida instantly started boiling up our sheets and towels in a frighteningly large iron pot that reminded me of a witch's cauldron. As the cottage was so small and our kitchen directly adjoined the living room the steam from the pot would come drifting in to where I was sitting and sometimes it gave me the sensation that I was being boiled alive with our household linen.

'I think I will just go down to the pub and pick up some cigarettes and see what's going on there,' I would say to my wife.

'Have a nice time, dearest,' Cressida would say as I left.

She never made me feel that she resented being left alone, that she found it churlish that I never urged her to join me. She made it obvious she had not the slightest desire to come with me to the Red Lion. She only wanted to stay at home and look after our child.

Mary Rose was six years old and Cressida had never gone out in the evenings since the day she was born. I once suggested that she get a babysitter and her pale eyes stared at me with such horror I realised she saw my suggestion as demonic.

'Leave a stranger in charge of a child!' she said.

'But if you found a nice reliable girl. If you found someone you could trust . . .' My protests sounded increasingly feeble.

'How can you ever trust a stranger?' Cressida's voice was husky with emotion. 'How can one ever be certain that any stranger is reliable, deep down?'

I could never win if I disagreed with Cressida. I never tried to. I preferred to bow politely to her curious logic. I could sometimes spend the whole day in her company and I often got the uneasy feeling that we were both together in the dark. It was as if I could feel my wife's presence without being able to see her. I was always intensely aware of her presence. She was so disconcertingly kind without warmth. She was so self-sacrificing and un-demanding and yet so stubbornly preoccupied with her own concerns.

As I said, the cottage was ill-lit even in the daytime, but when the natural light failed Cressida did her best to make the living room seem less gloomy. She switched on all the lamps and fed the log fire until the whole room was illuminated by the glorious flicker of its orange and scarlet flames. Yet despite the light of the lamps, and the fire, and the colour television, my feeling that we were both in darkness persisted.

Sometimes I tried to examine my wife when she was busy with some household task and I found myself squinting like someone in a darkroom who tries to make out an image in the negative of a photograph. I could just see she was beautiful but I couldn't see it plainly. My wife's blondness was ghostly. She was close to being an albino without having the white-lashed sickly rabbit-look that is the curse of many albinos. Cressida never dyed her hair but it had a salt-bleached brilliance like the hair of children on beaches. She made no effort to show off its silky beauty. She dragged it back behind her ears and pinned it in a bun as if it was something she wished to get rid of. She never wore any make-up. She had no interest in wearing pretty clothes. She wore jeans and plain brown shirts in the summer, and in the winter she wore jeans and plain brown shirts and heavy brown sweaters. Although Cressida was not in the least vain and took no trouble with her appearance she was still considered good looking. In the Red Lion people sometimes came up to me and said they had seen my beautiful wife taking a walk with my little girl. It always startled me when they said this since I had this unpleasant feeling she was shrouded in darkness. And yet I knew all too well that she had delicate features which looked as if they had been carved out of white marble. She had a slender and elegant figure. Her pale aquamarine eyes with their faraway trance-like stares were striking. She had a strained and melancholy expression as if she was nursing a secret sorrow and this gave her face an added mystery.

I have always had an aversion to cats. I accept that many people consider them to be beautiful animals but I remain blind to their beauty. I feel only disgust if some cat rubs itself against my leg – jumps on to my lap. I particularly dislike to stay in any house that has a cat that goes roaming around at night once all the lights are out. Cats move with such delicacy, perambulating too softly on their padded feline feet. Often only the tiniest squeak or rustle betrays their presence, yet their ceaseless nocturnal activity fills me with nervous alarm.

My wife in broad daylight gave me that same feeling of ill-ease. Cressida was always on the move. She did this.

18

She did that. She went from the larder to the kitchen, from the kitchen to the guest room, then back to the room she shared with Mary Rose. She moved with delicacy and grace. Her constant motion had superficial purpose. But what was she thinking about?

When she shortened Mary Rose's gymslip and the jarring whir of her sewing machine broke the silence in the cottage, could she be as totally absorbed by her task as she appeared to be? When she knelt beside my daughter's bed and dabbed away at the rug which had a dark patch where Mary Rose had spilt a glass of Ribena, could all Cressida's energies and intelligence really be concentrated on the removal of that blackcurrant stain?

Although my wife took impeccable care of my clothes when I stayed with her and buttons were sewn on my suits and my shirts were washed and pressed and starched every day, although my socks were darned and I was cosseted and indulged and only the most politely expressed disagreements marred our conjugal harmony, I had the feeling that I ceased to exist for my wife the very moment I left her cottage. She never asked me any questions about my life in London. She appeared to have no curiosity as to whom I saw there. She showed not the slightest interest in my work. She never telephoned me when I was in the city. About every ten days I rang her up. I asked her how she was. I inquired about Mary Rose. Cressida would then be polite but also quite curt. She always seemed anxious to cut short our conversation. She said she disliked talking to me long distance for she hated to feel she was wasting my money. If I told her I would not be able to see her for several weeks Cressida sounded disappointed, but again only very slightly disappointed. 'Well, I expect we shall see you sometime.' That was all Cressida ever said.

I used to wonder if my wife's excessive devotion to my comforts when I was staying under her roof sprang from her belief that as the perfect mother to Mary Rose it was her duty to let the child see her father treated with an exemplary and loving concern. I suspected that once I went to London and Mary Rose ceased to be a witness to the good-wifely role her mother enacted entirely for her benefit, I ceased to have the slightest value for my wife.

Cressida had always been curiously reticent about her own childhood. The pupils of her beautiful eyes shrank and she became evasive to the point of irritability whenever I questioned her about her parents, who were apparently both alive and living in Devonshire. As far as I knew she had never contacted them either by letter or by telephone. One Christmas I suggested she invite them to stay with her in Beckham. I said they might like to see their grandchild. My suggestion, although apparently genial and disinterested, had a secret selfish motivation. If Cressida's parents were to come to visit her there would not be enough room in the cottage for me to stay as well and I could then feel absolved of any guilty feeling that I ought to spend Christmas with my wife and Mary Rose. When I made the suggestion Cressida shook her blonde head with a jerk of uncharacteristic violence. 'My family can get along without me. And I can get along without them. I'm not a person who has ever needed company at Christmas or at any other time. The only family I care about is right here with me in Beckham.' I had no feeling that she included me in the family that she cared about – I knew she was referring only to Mary Rose.

Although I preferred to go to the pub rather than to remain in imaginary darkness with my wife, I never had a particularly enjoyable time once I got there. The Red Lion had a memorably vulgar décor. Its scarlet brothel-like walls had been festooned with brass warming-pans, studded horse collars and ancient ships' lanterns in an attempt to give it 'atmosphere', while its chromium bar was lit by the horrible sickly tubes of greenish fluorescent lighting that one sees in many modern offices. It was Beckham's most popular pub and it was therefore both over-heated and over-crowded and I usually found it impossible to find a seat.

I would stand by the bar looking sour and supercilious as I listened to the hearty guffaws of the stockbrokers, farmers and land agents who became increasingly red-faced and convivial as they consumed round after round of beer and spirits. It was the loudness of their laughter that mystified me. I wondered if they really found their own jokes as funny as they wanted to make it sound. Alcohol has never made me laugh. It tends to make me increasingly silent and morose. I therefore half envied, half resented, these men who found it easy to be so noisily amused.

Over the years I had visited the Red Lion quite frequently and I recognised a lot of the people who went there, but I had never managed to make any friends. I usually got into a desultory conversation with the landlord. He was an ex-army sergeant with a gingery handlebar moustache and intensely reactionary views. He would ask me how my wife was – how my little daughter was – 'She's very well . . . She's very well . . .' It was all like that.

Standing by the bar I picked up meaningless snippets of gossip. Someone's daughter had just got married . . . Someone else's brother-in-law was planning to respray his car . . . My eyes streamed as the pub filled with cigarette smoke. I was jostled. Beer was slopped on me. I heard complaints about the shocking price of brussels sprouts, more complaints about the price of petrol. 'It's all those bloody Arabs.'

Although the Red Lion 'regulars' enjoyed moaning about the rise of prices I was both puzzled and irrationally irritated by the way that the village of Beckham seemed to have retained an anachronistic prosperity in defiance of inflation and the national crisis and decline.

In the paranoid mood that came over me whenever I drank in the Red Lion's rowdy saloon bar I got the impression that almost everyone in the village had recently acquired either a microwave oven or the most expensive kind of modern freezer so that not one carrot or raspberry from their gardens would go to waste next summer. An astonishing number of families were planning to re-thatch the roofs of their ancient cottages despite the ever-rising cost of fire insurance. I noticed too that of the many cars that were parked outside the pub it was rare to see an old model. A couple of new bakeries were opening up near the village green just when I would have expected the existing bakery to be closing. The Red Lion itself, like the rest of the village, appeared to have put the clock back so successfully that it existed in an old fashioned never-never land where, seemingly untouched by the nation's financial predicament, its landlord still planned to build on a restaurant annexe where steaks would be served for lunch and dinner.

The evening that Maureen Sutton vanished from her house on the council estate Cressida started to become restless and peculiar. She seemed unable to concentrate on her ironing in her usual single-minded way. She continually left the living room and climbed the ladder staircase that led to the bedroom she shared with Mary Rose. She then returned to the living room where she kept turning the knob of the television as if desperately searching for some special channel, then, failing to find it, she went up again to see my sleeping daughter.

'What's the matter?' I asked her. 'Is Mary Rose feeling ill or something? Why do you keep going up to see her?'

'Mary Rose is asleep. She is safe in her bed.'

'You seem upset,' I said.

'Of course I'm upset,' Cressida answered. 'I can't bear to think of that little girl missing from her home. And the council estate is right near here.'

The council estate was certainly very near to our cottage. Although quick-growing trees had been planted in order to hide it, if you stood on Beckham's well-tended green the fringes of its garish public lavatory brick could be seen only too easily. When I went to the Red Lion I often heard it referred to as the 'eye-sore'. Cressida gave a fastidious little shudder of revulsion whenever it was men-

22

tioned. When I took Mary Rose out for a walk I was always irritated by the way she implored me not to take the child anywhere near the council estate. She behaved as if it was inhabited by ravening wolves who were waiting to leap on our daughter and devour her limb by limb.

Cressida loved Beckham for its immaculate daintiness. She loved it because water could still be drawn from its ancient well, because a weed was rarely to be seen on any of its tiny lawns. This made her feel she was bringing up our child in a decent community which still retained a proper respect for motherhood and property. She romanticised the past. She believed that everything had been better – once. It is common for people to dread the idea of change but I think that Cressida dreaded it more than most. She was comforted by the sight of the well-preserved little houses of Beckham because they provided her with tangible proof that certain things can survive the erosions of time and remain relatively unscathed.

Cressida saw the council estate as a threat. As I had never liked Beckham I couldn't care if it had been disfigured by the massive housing development that had been built on its outskirts. I felt there was something smug and tiresome in the way my wife deplored its existence. It was her exaggerated horror of it that made me feel perversely relieved that in the form of the council estate the modern world had arrived at Beckham's picture postcard gates, that it had arrived over-populated, poor and ill-planned with television sets with aerials that no one attempted to hide – aerials that stretched out their wiry arms as if in desperation they were seeking help from the sky.

'Why should they have bothered to report that that little girl is missing on the news?' Cressida asked me.

'Maybe they couldn't find anything more interesting to report?'

'You know that has to be nonsense, Rowan.' She spoke with unusual sharpness. 'You only have to read the newspapers to realise there is no shortage of horrible news. Just

23

read about India, about Africa, about the Middle East. Read about Ulster, that provides enough atrocious news in itself. Just read about anywhere . . .'

'I don't know what point you're trying to make.' I felt suddenly very tired. I only wanted to go to bed. I was longing to get back to London the next day.

'I'm trying to say that I feel certain the police must think something very serious has happened to that little girl.'

'I think you are reacting somewhat over-dramatically to the whole thing,' I said. 'Children are always disappearing from their homes and naturally the parents get very upset. The police are informed. Everyone starts to get in a big panic. The event gets into the newspapers – it even gets reported on the news. Then the missing child is found playing in the house of a school friend or something quite harmless like that.'

Cressida gave an impatient shrug. She held her lips tightly compressed as if she was trying to restrain herself from making some rude retort. Once again she climbed our terrible ladder staircase and I could hear her agitated footsteps through the ceiling as she moved around the bedroom where Mary Rose slept.

When she returned to the living room she said that our sleeping daughter looked so innocent she was like an angel. Cressida still appeared to be very tense and her pale eyes looked rather wild, and Mary Rose's angelic appearance didn't seem to have cheered her as much as I expected it to.

Out of politeness I said I wanted to go up to take a look at our child. I hoped my gesture would please Cressida but she hardly seemed to take it in. She turned on the television and said she wished to God she could get the news.

Having offered to look at Mary Rose sleeping, I went up to her room. Her bed was next to her mother's. Both beds looked equally small and for the first time I was struck by the fact that Cressida always slept in a child's bed.

24

Mary Rose was lying on her back with her mouth open. Her tiny stick-like arms were outstretched as if she was being crucified. She looked adenoidal and from time to time she moved her head restlessly as if she was having a bad dream.

When I went downstairs Cressida had started ironing again. I told her that I agreed with her, Mary Rose looked like a sleeping angel.

'That other child probably looked innocent too,' Cressida said grimly.

'Please don't work yourself up about that child,' I said. 'I think the whole thing has upset you because she lives so near – if you heard some child in Cumberland was missing from her home, you wouldn't be all that interested.'

'You are quite wrong.' Cressida stopped ironing. She looked wildly agitated and her pupils had shrunk and her eyes were like bits of aquamarine glass. There was something menacing in the way she held the steam iron.

'You are quite wrong,' she repeated. 'Even if I heard some child in Cumberland was missing it would haunt me. I wouldn't be able to stop thinking about all the ghastly things the child's mother must be going through.'

'I'm sure this one will turn up,' I said. 'Children often disappear and then they turn up safe and sound.'

'Sometimes they don't,' Cressida said. She started to fold her damp sheets. 'Sometimes they don't turn up safe and sound.'

Chapter Two

The night that little Maureen Sutton first started to haunt my household I stayed at home with my wife and child. The whisky Cressida had put out for me seemed to increase rather than cure my hangover. My head continued to ache so badly I wondered if I had migraine. My eyes were still stinging as if they had just been grazed by thorns.

As Cressida became increasingly fidgety and obsessed with the fate of the missing child I decided that it would be a very long time before I came down again to stay with her at the cottage.

Superficially my visit had been as calm and uneventful as usual, my relationship with my wife had been as civil as always. It still alarmed me that I remembered so little of what I'd done the previous evening. I had a hazy memory of tipping some roast duck that Cressida had cooked for my dinner down the lavatory and then setting off in my car for the Red Lion. But I had no recollection of being in the pub, nor could I remember leaving it. Presumably I'd managed to drive myself back to the cottage because my car was parked outside on the tiny gravel patio. At some point in the evening I had evidently taken a nasty fall because my hands were scratched and bloody and my suit was ripped and it had mud stains round the knees.

When I woke in the morning I found myself lying fully clothed on the sofa of Cressida's living room, where I must have passed out. I had not done this since I was an undergraduate and it shocked me.

Cressida was working away in the kitchen when I woke. She always got up at seven for she liked to make the cottage spotless before Mary Rose got up. When she came into the living room and found me lying in a dishevelled and wretched state on the sofa she behaved with her habitual poise. If she found me sordid and depressing, my face puffed up from over-drinking, my eyes bleary, my suit crumpled and stained, she showed no sign of disgust. When she examined me her pale aquamarine eyes looked through rather than at me. If for a moment she had abandoned her cool politeness and made some sarcastic contemptuous remark I would not have blamed her. Her conduct was, however, exemplary.

'Would you like me to run you a bath?' she asked me casually. 'I thought you might like to take one before I start getting you your breakfast.' Her offer sounded extremely friendly and helpful. However I knew it was really the politest possible way of telling me that she wanted to get me out of sight immediately. Mary Rose would be getting up at any moment. Mary Rose would be coming down to the living room. Cressida's only concern was to get me hidden away in the bathroom so I would not be seen by Mary Rose in an ill-kempt and semi-tipsy state.

I went and took a bath just as Cressida wanted me to. I shaved. I combed my hair. I changed my clothes. When I came down to the kitchen for breakfast I looked neat and presentable. I felt so ill that morning that the effort of going through these routine procedures was extremely painful to me. As I performed them I felt they might well be the supreme courtesy I had yet accorded my wife.

When I entered the kitchen my walk was brisk and my mood to all appearances was buoyant. I said good morning to my daughter and I gave her an affectionate hug. The child responded with no enthusiasm. But then she never did . . .

Mary Rose sat at the kitchen table with its gay red and white check tablecloth. She picked despondently at a bowl of Bemax, yeast and wheat germ. The bowl was decorated with colourful pictures of Peter Rabbit. 'Peter Rabbit is going to eat your lovely breakfast if you don't hurry up,' her mother said.

Cressida had put some daffodils in a vase in the centre of the table. The brilliance of these glorious yellow flowers seemed unpleasantly electric to me that morning. The golden blaze of their flaring petals hurt my sore eyes and I tried my best not to look at them. Symbols of spring, these daffodils presumably had been put on our breakfast table in order to give us all a feeling of renewal and hope.

Cressida was intent on making Mary Rose finish her health mixture so that she would grow up big and strong. Mary Rose kept choking as she miserably spooned down mouthful after mouthful of the pale brown slush her mother had put in her pretty bowl. When I looked at the child's breakfast it sickened me and I felt sorry for her. It reminded me of the bran mashes one sees offered in a bucket to a horse.

'I've had enough,' Mary Rose whispered plaintively. There was a note of desperation in her weak little voice. When she looked at the daffodils she didn't seem to see them. There was no sign that the sight of them cheered her up and gave her hope.

Cressida took the spoon from my daughter's hand and started to spoon-feed her as if she was an infant. Mary Rose slobbered and a trickle of slush ran down her chin. Cressida wiped it away with a napkin.

I longed for Mary Rose to scream, knock over the bowl, behave abominably. If only the child could have found the courage to show a sign of rebellion it is possible I might have protested against my wife's treatment of my daughter – asserted the paternal authority I'd never once chosen to assert since my daughter's birth.

If the child only could have cried out aloud for my help as she was spoon-fed her revolting mush of health food, it is just feasible that in the irritable and unthinking mood induced by my hangover I might have done what I'd sworn I'd never do. I might have tried to stop my wife tormenting the child with these spoonfuls of junk and Bemax. If I'd taken this step it would have been a momentous one in my relationship with Cressida, for if I'd found the energy openly to clash with my wife on this issue all the fragile barriers of our mutual politeness instantly would have crumbled.

I never took my daughter's side. I made no protest as I watched her being force-fed that nauseating mixture. I felt the wretched little girl ought to take the initiative before she could expect me to come to her aid. I was ashamed of my own passivity and by some intricate process of projection I felt profound contempt for the inertia of Mary Rose.

My little daughter looked exceptionally wan and spiritless that morning. It was a Sunday and the child was wearing her best dress and a snowy white cardigan because Cressida was soon going to take her to church. My wife was deeply religious although her faith was a topic that she had never discussed with me. This was just as well.

Cressida had put a bow in Mary Rose's hair that morning. I felt it looked a little silly. It was the sort of shiny bow that decorates chocolate eggs at Easter time. The ostentatious frivolity of this piece of bright ribbon only emphasised the limpness of the child's poor hair.

'Now say grace,' Cressida said. Mary Rose put her white stick-like fingers together in a pious gesture. She stumbled something unintelligible. I thought I heard the phrase 'Oh, beloved Father'.

My wife told her she could get down from the table and ordered her to wash her hands. 'And please make them thoroughly clean before you dry them. I don't want to find any sticky marks on the towels.'

The child left the breakfast table and trotted off like an obedient robot to the bathroom.

'Mary Rose is getting very grown up,' I said so as to avoid an uncomfortable silence.

'I worry about that child's future.' Cressida spoke with

such intensity that she startled me. It was the first time she had given me any hint that she was concerned about our daughter's future. Previously Cressida had always implied that she was confident Mary Rose would be for ever immune to the diverse problems that beset humanity because she had been blessed by an uniquely perfect upbringing.

*I wondered if Cressida could be starting to take a more realistic attitude towards Mary Rose. In the past, if she had admitted that the child suffered from certain disabilities, she had blamed them solely on extraneous factors. The child's abysmal academic record Cressida blamed on the low level of teaching at her school. According to my wife the classes Mary Rose attended were far too large and she was being denied enough individual care.

'Can any of the other children in her class read?' When I asked Cressida this question she became shifty and evasive. She never gave me any satisfactory answer.

Cressida did not deny that Mary Rose was physically delicate. For this she held the local doctor responsible. She claimed that the medical check-ups he gave the child were hurried and unsatisfactory and she had no faith in the accuracy of his diagnosis. The doctor had told my wife that Mary Rose was suffering from anaemia, and had prescribed her iron pills. Cressida was convinced that the child ought to be given an additional course of B 12 injections. She also had various other suggestions and remedies. She complained that the doctor became offhand and impatient to the point of rudeness when she tried to make him listen to her medical theories, and that he gave her the impression he longed to get her out of his office.

Cressida was convinced that Mary Rose's school lunches were nutritionally inadequate. She said the modern educational system paid far too little heed to the dietary needs of the growing child. 'All those terrible watery stews made of stock cubes and mutton fat – where is the goodness in that?' she'd say to me.

'Why are you worried about Mary Rose's future?' I

asked Cressida. She seemed to find it difficult to answer me. She was cooking some rashers of bacon for my breakfast and there was something hectic in the way she kept nervously spiking them with a large two-pronged kitchen fork. The very smell of Cressida's sizzling rashers made me feel sick that morning but I felt defeated and drained and, like my apathetic little daughter, I was prepared to let Cressida feed me what she wished. 'Is anything the matter with her?' I asked. I then added dishonestly, 'She seems so well.'

I noticed that Cressida's flaxen hair was scraped back from her pale face in a particularly severe and unflattering style. It was fastened in a pony tail which she was wearing tucked inside her brown sweater. It created a great bulge on her back which looked very curious. It was as if she had a deformity sprouting between her shoulder blades.

'It's not easy to bring up a child in the world we live in today.' My wife's voice was charged with emotion and she spoke so softly it was as if she was whispering some ghastly secret. Again she spiked the rashers with such roughness that they jumped around in the pan as if they were living things in pain. 'There's so much evil and violence about,' Cressida said.

'Surely there's not all that much evil and violence about here in Beckham.' My comment was jocular. Overtly it was reassuring. Only my habitual politeness prevented me from saying something much more caustic. I found it difficult to believe that this sleepy village had the alarming crime rate Cressida appeared to be insinuating it had. Doubtless there were a few delinquent teenagers in Beckham. Very possibly they occasionally stole a bicycle or a lawnmower. Most likely a certain number of hens mysteriously disappeared every year from Beckham's chicken runs and whether the theft was the work of humans or foxes it would be hard to say. Otherwise I assumed that the chief law breakers in the village were the vehicle owners with unpaid parking tickets – the television set owners with lapsed licences.

31

I felt that my wife was being both absurd and tedious when she claimed that she was bringing up Mary Rose in conditions of extreme adversity. From the way she spoke one would have thought that she and her child were battling for survival in some war-torn devastated country such as Uganda or Bangladesh.

When I said I failed to see that she was threatened by all that much evil and violence in Beckham, Cressida stopped browning the bacon and turned and glared at me. I saw that her pupils were starting to shrink. Her eyes looked both unseeing and visionary.

'Where you find people you will always find evil and violence,' she muttered.

'Oh, Cressida . . . Please . . . I'd like to know how you hope to avoid people. Are you planning to bring up Mary Rose on some uninhabited island in the Indian Pacific?'

'That might be much better.' Cressida didn't smile. She was devoid of humour.

'There's only one thing that I pray for Mary Rose,' she said.

'And what's that?' I found this discussion increasingly futile and dreary. I wished that Cressida would take Mary Rose off to church. I longed to be alone. I wanted to go upstairs and collapse on my bed. I needed to take some aspirin and Alka-Seltzer. I foresaw a foolishly wasted day which would be devoted to futile attempts at recuperation. I would lounge around all morning, read the Sunday papers my wife had gone out thoughtfully to buy for me. At lunch-time I'd try gallantly to force down some of Cressida's Sunday roast and her homemade apple pie. After lunch, while Cressida took my daughter for a healthy walk and made her attend Sunday school, I'd go back to bed. Cressida with typical tact no doubt would tell Mary Rose that her father was suffering from a bout of 'flu.

Around six I'd come down to watch the television and drink some of the whisky that I'd find my wife had laid out for me. The day that stretched before me seemed unappealing in the extreme. All I saw as important was that when evening came I resist the temptation to go to the Red Lion. I knew it was vital that I retire early and sleep off my hangover so that when I returned to London the next morning I would have some hope of feeling sane and well and ready to resume work.

'There is only *one* thing that I pray for Mary Rose.' Cressida spoke with dramatic emphasis. I think she sensed my attention was wandering, that whatever it was that she prayed for my daughter, it in no way intrigued me as much as she thought it should. It occurred to me that if anyone were to ask me what I would pray for Mary Rose I'd be unable to give them any answer at all.

Cressida suddenly stopped browning the rashers. She held up her double-pronged kitchen fork as if it were a trident. 'I pray this,' she said. 'I've taught Mary Rose many things. But all I pray is that I've managed to teach her the only thing that matters.'

'What's that?' I asked. I was hoping that as Cressida became increasingly absorbed in this unrewarding conversation she might forget to finish cooking me my bacon and so I wouldn't feel forced to eat it.

'There is only one thing that I pray that Mary Rose has learned from me. I pray I've taught her to know the difference between right and wrong.'

I nodded politely. I made no comment. When my wife made these unanswerable statements all light seemed to vanish from the cottage and I felt we were both groping about hopelessly in the dark.

Chapter Three

I kept my resolution that night. At about 8.30 I told Cressida that I had a headache and I was going up to bed.

'Well, I do hope you sleep well!' my wife muttered with such a snapping and uncharacteristic bitterness that she made it sound like a curse. I realised that it was only her fear of seeming intrusive which prevented her from telling me directly that she felt I was being callous in retiring so early. She was obviously profoundly shocked that I didn't want to stay up with her in order to see if there was any further report on the fate of the missing child.

In retrospect I think I probably should have stayed up as she wanted me to. But that evening I felt raw and irritable and my exhaustion was not only physical, it was spiritual. I therefore ignored my wife's unspoken plea. I merely told Cressida in oily tones that I hoped she would sleep well too.

Once I was in bed, tired as I was, I still found it hard to sleep. Cressida's guest room was cramped and stuffy. Its latticed window was so tiny it seemed almost non-existent. There was a great black painted beam that slanted down from the ceiling at such a threatening angle it cut the small room in two.

Cressida had done her best to make her guest room pretty and pleasant. The bed was covered by a patchwork quilt which she had made herself. It had taken her weeks to make, but although it was decorative and beautifully made, I still felt it had been a waste of her time. I could have bought her an antique quilt if she had asked me for it.

Even that would have been pointless. Apart from myself Cressida had never once had a guest to stay with her in the cottage. I didn't care what kind of cover Cressida put on my bed, so I could have been provided with a tatty blanket or some priceless antique and it would have seemed equally sad and unimportant.

Cressida had put a vase of daffodils on my bedside cabinet. I tried to feel grateful for her gesture, I tried to see it as touching, but like the bright flowers she had put on our breakfast table, the sight of them was disturbing to me and I would have preferred it if they weren't there.

I finally turned out the lamp which had a parchment shade that Cressida had decorated with a stencil design of small red roses. The mattress of the bed was much too soft and I tossed about, feeling too depressed after a day in which I'd accomplished nothing of the slightest value, to find the relaxation that is necessary to me before I can sleep.

Gloria was always telling me that she thought my visits to my family were ludicrous. 'What exactly do you think they accomplish?' she would scream at me.

I became stubbornly defensive when Gloria attacked me on this subject. I told her I wished to keep up some personal contact with my daughter, that I failed to understand why she found this in any way abnormal. I was just as dishonest with Gloria as I was with my wife whenever I spoke of my feelings for Mary Rose. The more I claimed to be deeply attached to the child, the more I wished that it was true.

Gloria never for a moment believed that I went down to Kent because I was devoted to Mary Rose. She was ferociously jealous of my wife and she was convinced that I was in love with her. Gloria had never met my wife but she had come across a snapshot of her amongst the papers in one of my drawers, and my wife's beauty had terrified and shocked her. When I examined the snapshot that Gloria found so disturbing I could see that my wife might seem threatening if you saw her as a rival. She certainly looked very lovely standing in front of her ancient cottage which was covered in a flowering tangle of wistaria, cyclamen and roses. Even the cottage looked attractive in the snapshot . . . For once Cressida was wearing her hair loose and it hung down her shoulders, sun-lit like the hair of a princess in a fairy tale. Her delicate oval face was pale and ethereal. Somehow Cressida looked immensely vulnerable standing there alone in front of her doorway clutching the infant Mary Rose protectively to her breast as if she saw the camera as an instrument that threatened her beloved infant. Her vulnerability added to the haunting glamour of her image.

Ever since Gloria had come across this snapshot she had always referred to my wife as 'that wretched woman', and she became obsessed by trying to stop me from going down to the cottage. As I've already said, the visits I made my wife were becoming increasingly infrequent but this did not placate Gloria. It enraged her that I still made any visits at all.

When I got back to London after having spent a couple of days at the cottage, Gloria inevitably threw a violent tantrum. She would have sobbing fits and berate me all through the night. Hairbrushes, shoes and various other objects were hurled at me across the bedroom. She accused me of being a heartless and exploitative bastard. Gloria's invective was vitriolic and finally I would lose my temper. I told her to get out of my flat. I said I had no intention of letting her rule my life. If I chose to see my wife and child no one was going to stop me. If she didn't like it that was unfortunate. Our quarrels usually ended by my telling Gloria she was a boring bitch and I didn't care if I never saw her again. Gloria always left my flat crying and cursing me. Fortunately she had a flat of her own. She frequently told me that she wanted to give it up. She complained it was an idiotic waste of money, paying the rent when she spent so much time in mine. I was, however, adamant that she keep it on. Her flat was an air-hole that stopped me from suffocating. Gloria was so

36

possessive that I needed to have the feeling that I could terminate our rocky relationship the very instant it became insufferable to me.

The rows I had with Gloria whenever I visited Cressida followed a pattern that was ritualistic and predictable to the point of tedium. The mutual insults we exchanged were like tennis balls that were volleyed backwards and forwards as part of a formal game. When at a certain point I asked Gloria to leave my flat and told her that I hoped never to see her again I knew as she left with her suitcase, spitting with fury and saying she hated me more than she had ever hated any other human being, that in the morning she would telephone me and apologise. I also knew that I'd immediately apologise in my turn for all the abusive things I had said to her. We would then meet for lunch in some restaurant and drink a lot of wine and brandy and after that we would go back to my flat and make love.

Although Gloria's childish and aggressive outbursts were much more comprehensible to me than the uncaring subservience to which I was subjected by Cressida, I still found Gloria's jealous scenes emotionally draining. Even after our ritual reconciliations had been completed I was left with a residue of resentment. Gloria knew nothing of the circumstances of my marriage. They were painful to me and I had therefore never discussed them with her. I see now that this was cruel and that if I had not been so tantalisingly reticent, if I had only given her an honest picture of my loveless relationship with Cressida, all her fears could have been easily dispelled. However, I chose to let Gloria torture herself and I endured her tantrums and rages because I wanted her to realise that there were areas of my life that I wished her neither to understand nor control.

Gloria often claimed half jokingly that she suffered from an 'empress complex', that ever since she was a very small girl she had gone through life with a feeling that she was wearing an imaginary crown upon her head.

I asked her if her phantom crown ever created any difficulties for her when she was dealing with the common people. Gloria laughed and confessed that in the past many of her relationships had come to grief because her lovers had failed to realise they were dealing with a ruling monarch, and had tried to treat her as if she was simply Gloria Walker from Surrey.

'An empress cannot tolerate many of the things that other people are prepared to put up with,' Gloria explained to me. 'An empress feels that because of the exalted nature of her role, she has been selected by destiny to enjoy every possible privilege. An empress demands total submission and devotion from those around her. An empress cannot take the slightest jolt for her imperial pride is very easily offended and she will always wreak ruthless vengeance on anyone who makes her feel that her crown is tipping over her nose.'

'In other words,' I said, 'an empress is a total nightmare.'

Gloria laughed. 'In some ways she might be called that,' she said. 'But you ought to sympathise with the problems of self-anointed empresses. Life is harder for them than it is for the major part of humanity. It's exhausting always having to assert imperial authority.'

I once asked Gloria to give me an example of how empresses behaved differently from the average person.

'Well, for one thing,' Gloria said, 'no one with an empress complex can ever be made to wait.'

'Wait for what?' I asked.

'Wait for anything. Surely you can understand that empresses must *not* be made to wait. For example any empress has to be made love to the very second *she* feels like it. She can't possibly be made to wait until the man feels like it. No empress is prepared to tolerate that kind of waiting at all . . .'

Although Gloria enjoyed making mock of her complex and often joked about it, I felt wary of the dominating aspects of her nature and I was always struggling to prevent Gloria from turning me into one of her humble subjects.

Gloria was very attractive. She was also quite vain. She was humorous, energetic and sharp-tongued. She earned large sums of money working as a freelance fashion model. She was also a competent journalist and she wrote travel articles, book reviews and she interviewed celebrities. She was quite a skilled photographer and she had produced a clever book of photographs of animals. She had never had any dramatic training but because of her beauty she had been given several small parts in television plays.

Gloria was immensely ambitious. She was unfortunate in this respect for her ambitions were hopelessly diffused. She longed for fame without ever having precisely decided what she wanted to be famous for. On one level she would have liked to have been a famous novelist, a modern Jane Austen, a slyly perceptive observer of contemporary manners and values. This ambition seemed doomed to failure for the chapters of Gloria's astonishing novel remained in her head while her articles entitled 'Does the pill hurt your sex life?' and 'Where to eat in Cyprus' appeared from time to time in glossy magazines.

Gloria would have also liked to be a celebrated actress on the level of Duse and Bernhardt.

'Why don't you take acting lessons?' I asked her.

Gloria shrugged. Although her fantasies were often ludicrously impractical, she could be realistic. 'I'm afraid I haven't got either the talent or the stamina,' she said sadly. 'And anyway I've left it too late. I'm already far too old.'

Gloria also had less lofty ambitions. She had moods when she wanted to be famous as an international beauty. She would have liked to have been photographed with prominent movie stars in the exclusive nightclubs of New York, London and Paris – gossiped about in news columns, listed as one of the best dressed women in the world. Although this aspiration was more likely to be realised than her dreams of becoming a world famous actress or novelist, Gloria never achieved it all the same. She was quite well known in the London fashion world but she never became celebrated internationally for her beauty. Maybe at heart she was insufficiently worldly to wish to devote her life to becoming a much publicised jet-set beauty and doing all the dreary things that this must entail.

Maybe it was Gloria's inner feeling that she was an unrecognised royalty that made her think at certain moments that her ambitions would only find fulfilment if she were to make a spectacular and brilliant marriage. She saw herself as the wife of some famous scientist, artist or politician. When she was indulging in this particular fantasy Gloria felt she deserved to be the wife of Picasso – if only he hadn't died – or of J. F. Kennedy, if only he hadn't been shot.

Although Gloria's free-floating ambitions could make her seem schoolgirlish and silly, she could also be ruthlessly self-critical. She suffered from bouts of self-disgust and depression. She often told me that she felt she had wasted her life, that she had accomplished nothing of any importance and she was never going to do so. She felt she was getting old. (Gloria was twenty-six.) She was losing her looks. She was tired of drifting around on the fringes on the fashion world. She wanted to have something in her life that was real. She would like to have a baby before it was too late. She hated the aridity of casual love affairs. She felt it was time she settled down. In these deflated moods all her conceits and confidence vanished and she lowered her sights drastically. She no longer wanted to make a dazzling marriage. She wanted to marry me.

But I already had a wife who had settled down. I already had a child and I had no desire to have another one. When Gloria tried to make me marry her I felt only panic.

I was terrified that if Gloria were to become pregnant she would behave like Cressida and persuade me to buy her a cottage in the country where she could bring up our child in peaceful surroundings far from the corruption and fumes of the city. I could already visualise Gloria's future cottage with painful clarity; it was almost identical to Cressida's and situated in some village very similar to Beckham but in a different county.

If I were to get a divorce and marry Gloria and she were to settle down and have a child by me, I would still have to support Cressida and Mary Rose. The prospect of maintaining two separate country establishments in addition to my London flat was horrendous to me. However many dream cottages I had the misfortune to acquire I was determined that my life must on no account change. I wanted to continue to live in my flat. It was pleasant and functional and it contained my library and my collection of classical records and it was a place where I liked to work.

Gloria often complained that she hated trundling backwards and forwards between our two flats, that her make-up and her clothes always seemed to be in the wrong place. She said that the way I made her live was unnatural and inconvenient and was putting a strain on our relationship. I never agreed with her although obviously Gloria suffered from the inconvenience of our living arrangements much more than I did. My flat is very small. It is suitable for only one person. Gloria had a huge wardrobe and there was no space for her to hang all her clothes. She always came round to my flat in the evenings. I never went round to hers. When I woke in the morning, I woke in a place where I wanted to be. All I had to do was make some coffee and I could immediately start work. When Gloria woke, she found herself in a place from which she was soon to be evicted. She knew that she'd have to go out in the street to get a taxi or a bus to get back to her own flat. Quite often she had nothing to put on except for the things she had worn the previous evening. Evening clothes look foolish in daylight and Gloria complained she felt idiotic standing at a bus stop in the rain wearing some long flowing dress, an embroidered ornamental cloak and delicate golden shoes.

I suppose I could have slept in Gloria's flat sometimes but I never felt comfortable there. It had been done up by an interior decorator and was self-consciously modern and chic. It seemed more like a showpiece that had been designed to display how one could live in a stylish décor than a place where one was meant to live.

Gloria's flat reflected neither her taste nor her personality. None of its contents was precious to her. They were there only because her decorator had chosen them. She didn't particularly like her flat and she would have been happy to sell it overnight if she could have moved into mine. I was fond of my little flat and it would have been painful to me if I'd been forced to leave it. I therefore felt that we might as well sleep in a place that was liked at least by one of us. Gloria thought my attitude selfish and she resented me for it. She said she loathed leading the life of a commuter. But if she had moved in with me as she wanted, I doubt if our relationship would have survived more than a week.

Gloria could never understand it but there are certain stages when I am working when I need to be alone in the fundamental way that I need air to breathe. At such times I find the presence of any other human being intolerable. For days I become so immersed in the period that I am researching that I feel I'm living in the present only as a technicality. At such times I neglect myself. I neither shave nor wash. I keep odd hours. I read most of the night. If the telephone rings, I refuse to answer it. I hardly eat. By neglecting my current needs I get the sense that I am relinquishing my identity which frees me to identify more fully with the lives of the characters I am writing about, to think their thoughts, experience what they experienced. For obvious reasons these cerebral flights from the present can only be made if I am completely alone. I want no one to distract me and bring me back to the life I have temporarily abandoned.

Gloria was always unhappy and angry in these periods

42

when I holed myself up in my flat and made no contact with her for several weeks. She felt I was rejecting her, which was true, though my rejection was in no way personal, and this she failed to see. Gloria was incapable of being alone for a moment. She needed the constant approval of others and without it she wilted like a flower deprived of water. As the desire for solitude was incomprehensible to her, when I shut myself up she suspected me of treachery and infidelity. When she couldn't reach me on the telephone, she became convinced that I had another woman living with me in the flat. Sometimes she thought I had secretly left London and had gone down to the cottage to be with Cressida. Once when I was immersed in a spell of highly concentrated work and had neither seen nor spoken to anyone for several days, I was walking up and down my flat thinking and I happened to glance out of the window. I saw that a woman was standing outside on the pavement and she was gazing up at my building. I pulled myself out of my trance-like state and as my mind returned with difficulty to reality I realised with horror that the woman in the street was Gloria. She was spying on me. I dread to think how long she had been out there standing in the street. I never found out for I chose never to mention I'd seen her there. I saw her behaviour as lacking in dignity and it sickened me. I've no idea how much time Gloria spent keeping watch on my building. I have the horrible suspicion she often spied on me all through the night. After I'd once become aware of her embarrassing espionage I was careful never again to look out of my window. If Gloria was out there in the street, I didn't want to know.

I sometimes wondered whether I would have remained married to Cressida if Gloria had not tried so hard to persuade me to divorce her. Gloria continually made jeering references to my marriage. She enjoyed pointing out its glaring defects. As I was much more aware of the shortcomings of my marriage than Gloria ever could be, when she insulted Cressida I felt only a perverse feeling of gratitude towards my pale strange wife. At least Cressida did exactly what she wanted and in her turn allowed me the perfect freedom to do the same. I always thought about Cressida with much more warmth when I was in London than when I was alone with her in the cottage. When I was away from her I saw her as having a certain gallantry. She led a stark restricted lonely life with Mary Rose but she never gave a hint that she held me responsible for its hardship. Although Cressida was financially dependent on me, emotionally she was not in the least parasitical. She wanted neither my time nor my affection, whereas Gloria was always asking me for more of both than I was prepared to give.

Somewhere at the centre of Gloria's life I sensed there was an emptiness and that frightened me. Gloria was ebullient and popular. Superficially she was much more at ease and successful than Cressida, but she was not self-sufficient. She dabbled in journalism, she dabbled with photography and fashion but she lacked any real passion or direction. She had the illusion that marriage could supply her with the sense of purpose that she lacked and this, I felt, was extremely dangerous.

Just as I might well have left Cressida if I'd not needed my marriage as a bulwark against Gloria's imperialism, I think that Gloria with her ambitious nature might very well have left me if I had not insisted on staying married to Cressida. I never felt it was my love that Gloria wanted. It was more complicated than that. Although she was unaware of it I think she was really always battling to get the love that she imagined I felt for Cressida. Her competitive energies were continually goaded by her failure to capture something that was bound to elude her as it existed only in her imagination.

'Why do you let yourself be so dominated by that wretched woman?' Gloria often shouted. 'You are such a weak character. You seem to be terrified of that stupid blonde bitch. She obviously has some kind of hold over you.'

I responded by becoming odious, cynical and shrugging, which only served to increase Gloria's conviction that there was some mysterious mutual attraction between Cressida and myself which I was trying to hide from her.

'Cressida is a very good wife,' I'd say casually. 'Why should I divorce her?'

'A good wife!' Gloria always then exploded. 'My God, you are an arrogant bastard. Your idea of a good wife is a wife that you never see!'

'I do see her.' When Gloria became too strident I could never resist saying the thing that was the most calculated to needle her.

'Oh yes, indeed!' Gloria's face always became so red when she was taunted that I'd sometimes wonder if she was going to have a stroke. 'The miserable creature gets a visit from you once every six weeks if she is lucky. I suppose you think she ought to be contented with that!'

'Cressida is contented with that.' When I told Gloria the truth, it often sounded untrue.

There were often dizzying moments in my quarrels with Gloria when she would turn round and side with Cressida and accuse me of neglecting and maltreating her. 'That wretched woman can't be happy,' she'd tell me. 'Her life must be hell stuck away all alone in the country with a small whining child.'

'Cressida is very attached to the child.'

'No doubt she is. That's not the point. Her life still isn't natural. It's not natural for a young woman of her age to live without any sex.'

'How do you know she doesn't have any sex?' I was being cruel. I knew it always traumatised Gloria if I even mildly insinuated that I slept with Cressida when I visited the cottage. The idea that I still had any sexual relations with my wife upset Gloria to the point that she became hysterical. She had a wildly inaccurate picture of my wife. She saw her as a luscious irresistible siren; alternatively as an evil all-powerful witch. In both the roles that Gloria

45

ascribed to Cressida, she invested my wife with insidious, superhuman powers of sexuality. She then became frantic, feeling her inability to compete with this mythical and forbidding female that she alone had invented.

Sometimes I saw Gloria like a great bull that kept charging my life and forcing me to side-step with as much of the matador's skill as I could muster. But there were times when I behaved without the beautiful finesse that mitigates the cruelty of the bullfighter. When I drew blood I felt more like a clumsy butcher. One night I was lying in bed with Gloria. We had had a pleasant evening. We had seen a good film and dined in an Italian restaurant. There had been no disputes. Gloria was at her most charming and affectionate. She was lying with her head on my chest. Her inky black hair smelled of almonds. She stroked my body and I was enjoying the feathery and electric feeling of her fingers. 'If we ever have a child,' she whispered amorously, 'I hope that it looks like you.' I had some kind of seizure. My behaviour was inexcusable. I pushed Gloria's head off my chest with such a violent gesture of revulsion that she gave a little scream. For a flashing second I had a vivid image of Mary Rose, I saw her wan dispiriting little face. Her nose was running. 'I don't want to have a child!' I screamed at Gloria. 'Why the hell should you think I want to have a child by you?'

Afterwards I felt I'd savaged her with a meat cleaver. I wanted to apologise but I felt I'd been so needlessly cruel and insulting that my behaviour was beyond apology. She didn't speak one word for the rest of the night. I wished she would berate me. But she remained mute. She seemed confounded by the aggression I'd shown her. I think she knew we had touched upon an issue over which we could never quarrel lightly as if our fighting was part of a game.

Gloria turned her back on me. She went under the bedclothes and she lay there miserably in a hump. I wanted to put my arm around her but I found I simply couldn't bring myself to do it. After the gratuitously savage thing I'd just said to her, I thought she'd feel that any conciliatory gesture would be corrupt.

All night I asked myself the same nagging questions. 'What makes me do it?' 'What makes me feel that I have to be so cruel?'

In the morning I was much nicer to Gloria than usual. Instead of making it obvious that I wanted her to go so that I could get to work, I suggested we drive out to the country and have a picnic. It was a beautiful spring day. Every square and garden in London was bright with blossom. Gloria looked so pale I was worried that she was getting ill. She didn't seem very excited by the idea of the picnic but she went off to the local supermarket to buy salami, cheese and French bread. We drove out to the country and picnicked in an idyllic spot by a river. Our conversation was stiff. We were shy as if we were strangers. There was not much gaiety in our picnic.

As I drove back to London with Gloria sitting silent and still crushed beside me I felt that I deserved to be married to Cressida. I couldn't hurt my wife. She was much too well-armoured. Her indifference protected her like a suit of chain-mail. Cressida was prepared to treat me with a chilly civility because I supported her but she always gave me the feeling that if I were to drop down dead in her cottage, it wouldn't ruffle her. She'd be anxious to get my body removed as quickly as possible. She'd be worried that the sight of it would be frightening and upsetting to our daughter. Once she'd seen to it that I was decently disposed of her thoughts would be practical. She'd hope that I'd left a will that made provision for Mary Rose.

I could never hurt Cressida because I existed for her only as a convenient puppet. She manipulated me with such delicacy and adroitness that I was often hardly aware of the subtlety of her manipulations. Superficially she seemed to ask for so little and whatever she asked from me was only by implication for she was far too proud to make overt demands. Cressida was like a fund-raiser. When she rattled her tin box she rattled it discreetly and she collected only for her cause. She saw every penny she

47

got from me as honourably acquired. She never felt she was collecting for herself. She did it only for Mary Rose.

The night I slept so badly on the over-soft mattress in Cressida's guest room I realised that I wanted to divorce her. Important decisions can sometimes be made with such suddenness that one gets the feeling that the decision has made itself and one has had almost no part in it. Previously I had persuaded myself there was little point in putting an end to the farce of my marriage. I'd always claimed that it harmed no one, that its negative aspects suited Cressida just as they suited me. Tossing around in the guest room while my wife fussed about downstairs by the television waiting for news of the missing child, I felt I had been duping myself for the last six years. Emotional inertia had made me overlook an important fact. Our sham marriage was not particularly destructive to Cressida. As I felt that I was often brutal in my relationship with Gloria I'd been far too pleased with this. The thing I'd never chosen to face was that this hollow and hypocritical marriage was becoming increasingly destructive to me. Cressida felt no need to get stupidly drunk when I visited her. Cressida coolly played the role of the loving submissive wife and if the act she was prepared to put on was entirely fraudulent she gave no sign that this disturbed her. As far as Cressida was concerned the charade of amicable domesticity we both enacted when we were together was a charity performance. She felt the proceeds were going to a valuable cause, which for her was Mary Rose.

I wondered if I ought to get up and go downstairs to tell Cressida that I wanted a divorce. How would she react? Would she behave in the agreeable offhand way she behaved when I told her I was going out to the pub? Once I had politely reassured her that in the future I intended to support my daughter and herself in the same style to which they were accustomed, I couldn't believe that she would find my wish for divorce all that devastating. I kept trying to find the most courteous reason to explain why I suddenly wanted to break up our marriage. Should I say that I had found another? Was that polite or insulting? As our marriage superficially had run so smoothly because it had been oiled by mutual civility, I felt it was appropriate that it should end on a civil note.

Was it possible to persuade Cressida that I wanted a divorce because I felt it would be better for Mary Rose? Gloria in fact had often told me that she thought it must be confusing for my daughter to have an absentee father who made occasional visits to the cottage during which he put on a show of paternal affection and then vanished again without explanation.

I myself felt that Gloria was probably right although my wife maintained that my visits were immensely important to Mary Rose. Whether my wife believed this or only said it to be polite to me, I couldn't tell. I assumed that I would find out how she really felt about it when I asked her for a divorce. If she genuinely believed my visits were valuable to the child, presumably she would put pressure on me to persuade me to continue to come down to the cottage after our marriage ended.

I decided that night in Cressida's guest room that when I asked her for a divorce, I would be telling her that I never wished to return to her claustrophobic cottage. I felt this last visit had been so disastrous that I couldn't believe my unfortunate little daughter would suffer all that much if she was never to see me again.

What use had I been to her? This weekend I had brought her a large plastic doll that could both cry and pee. She had thanked me because my wife had prompted her to do so. Quite rightly she had given no sign that she was at all excited by my gift. I noticed that she made no attempt to play with it. She immediately left it abandoned on a chair in our living room. It still lay there looking obscene with its shiny pink and dimpled thighs spread wide apart to show the white piece of towelling on which it was meant to wet itself. I rather admired Mary Rose for

49

instantly rejecting the synthetic baby I'd presented her with. If she'd cradled it and cooed, if she'd fed the silly object its plastic bottle and burped it on her shoulder, it would have made me very uneasy. Mary Rose clearly had no desire to take a maternal role towards the wretched doll and her behaviour, unlike that of her father, was entirely consistent with her feelings.

Thinking about my daughter's reaction to my gift, it occurred to me that she rarely played like other children. My wife gave her books to colour and for hours she would sit at a table very quietly filling in the illustrations with crayons. But she occupied herself as if she was completing a necessary dull task rather than deriving any particular pleasure from her activity. My wife gave her picture books to look at and this also kept the child quiet. As Mary Rose couldn't read she turned the pages mechanically and stared dumbly at the illustrations. She never commented on them. They never seemed to interest her. It was as if she looked at them without seeing them. Her attention appeared to be elsewhere. But what she was ever really thinking about I found it impossible to tell.

Mary Rose rarely played but at least she refused to play act and thinking about her that night I felt this gave the child a certain dignity. If I told my wife the time that I would be arriving at the cottage, Cressida made Mary Rose stand at her bedroom window so that she could wave to me when she saw my car arriving. The way my daughter flicked her skinny little white wrist when she saw my car scrunching up the gravel was so unenthusiastic that sometimes I felt she was gesturing for me to go away rather than showing signs of welcome. I occasionally wondered if my child disliked me more than I cared to realise. Sometimes I thought I saw an expression which was near to one of hatred in her tiny lack-lustre eyes. I never knew if I was imagining this, whether I was merely projecting on to the unfortunate Mary Rose feelings that the guilt I felt towards her made me think she ought to feel. Certainly if it was detestation I saw in the little girl's expression, like unshed tears it only remained trapped in her eyes. She never once showed any overt hostility towards me. But then aggression was a quality that Cressida seemed to have wrung out of the child in much the same way as my wife with her strong chapped hands wrung soiled water from the kitchen mop.

The night that I first fully realised how much I wanted to divorce Cressida, I felt I'd been fortunate not to have had a nasty accident the previous evening. It horrified me to think I had driven in such a disgustingly drunken state. If I'd crashed into something or run over some old lady and been had up for manslaughter and drunken driving, it would have been extremely destructive to Cressida and Mary Rose. In the small and gossipy community of Beckham it would have created an immense scandal. My wife would have found this agonising. Above all things she wanted me to present a respectable image in her village. She longed for my reputation to be spotless because I was the father of Mary Rose.

By sheer good luck. I had not hurt anyone as I drove home but I still doubted that my behaviour in the Red Lion had been such that it would make my family feel proud. I could only pray that I had not insulted anyone. I had the horrible feeling that I could easily have behaved abominably last night because I'd used alcohol to push myself into a state that was closer to that of psychosis than routine drunkenness. I very much suspected that that explained why my memory had blocked out all trace of the evening. Unconsciously I must have felt that for a few hours I needed to go dangerously out of control. I needed to give myself such a fright that I could no longer avoid facing the fact that various steps had to be taken in my life if there was not to be a repetition of this degrading and self-destructive episode. Obviously the most vital step was to divorce Cressida and wriggle out of the trap of my disheartening marriage. If the strain of visiting Cressida had become intolerable and I could only deal with it by getting dangerously drunk it was obviously better for all of us if my visits were to cease. All this seemed clear as I lay awake in my wife's guest room. But I continued to worry that the events of the night before still remained unclear. I couldn't bear the way that when I tried to reconstruct the previous night's visit to the Red Lion, my memory became like a slimy and ink-black lake in which things stirred and rippled as if they were about to rise to the surface and yet remained tantalisingly submerged. I decided it was useless to torment myself by trying to remember this lost evening. I must think of the future and make plans for my divorce.

Chapter Four

I had bad dreams that night. I dreamt I had lost an important reference book. I didn't know its title but its loss was a nightmare. I woke shivering and it took me a long time to get back to sleep. When I finally dozed off again, I dreamt about Mary Rose's doll. It was lying on an operating table. Doctors were standing round it, their faces half-covered by white masks. Their eyes looked grim. The doll's legs were wide apart and kicking in the air. It was wearing a white piece of towelling. I saw the towelling was stained with blood as if the doll was menstruating. The doctors stamped their feet on a floor of marble. The sinister sound of their rhythmic stamping terrified me. Again I woke and my heart was pounding.

To my horror, the noise didn't stop. It continued softly but relentlessly. I lay in bed and wondered if all the alcohol I had drunk in the last couple of days had affected my brain. Then I realised that someone was tapping on my door and the sound filled me with dread. For a moment I thought a burglar had broken into the cottage. As I became more wide awake, I realised this idea was ludicrous. Why would a burglar knock on a door? The person who was tapping had to be Cressida.

The reason I was so slow to realise that it was my wife at my door was that since we had bought the cottage, Cressida had never once come near my bedroom at night. It was so unlike her to disturb me once I'd gone to bed that I was alarmed. I thought she must be ill.

I sometimes wondered if Cressida stayed up boiling

sheets so late into the night only out of consideration. If she pretended that she had urgent housework that was going to keep her up, it made it less tense and embarrassing for both of us when we had to say good night. When I didn't go out to the Red Lion I was always the one who retired first. Once Cressida thought I was asleep, she slipped discreetly up to the bedroom she shared with Mary Rose.

Love didn't die in our marriage. Love couldn't die, because love was never born. I first met Cressida when she was working in a florist's shop which was near my flat in Notting Hill Gate. I had just started my affair with Gloria and I wanted to send her some flowers. I had offended her the night before and she had walked out of the restaurant where we were dining in a rage. At the time I felt only relief as she flounced out. I was glad to be left alone so that I could go back to my flat and continue working on a review of a dull, ill-written book that dealt with the decline of religion in urban societies. I didn't feel I had been offensive to Gloria and her histrionic exit struck me as self-important and maddening. The next day, having finished the review, I decided to send her some flowers. I had found the article difficult to write. It was not on a subject that interested me and I wished that I'd never agreed to do it. I had gone out to dinner in an irritable mood, leaving a half finished piece which I was far from satisfied with. In retrospect I realised that I had been unfair to Gloria. All through dinner I had been morose and preoccupied. I'd talked about myself continually and had been such poor company that I now felt Gloria had been right to take umbrage and leave the restaurant the way she had. I wanted to send her flowers as my apology for having been self-obsessed and boorish.

Gloria used to claim that contrition was my speciality – that the morning after I'd behaved revoltingly I operated like an emotional con artist. She said I was an expert at begging for forgiveness and adored appearing with champagne and flowers as a peace offering – that I deliberately put on an irresistibly sheepish little boy grin. Although it is true that I like to make reparation if I feel I have upset someone, when I make conciliatory gestures I never feel they are as perfidious as Gloria chose to believe. The truth is that I am often unaware of how offensive my moods of excessive self-absorption can seem to other people and it is only when I think about my behaviour on the following day that I can see it in perspective. I then feel genuine remorse, which Gloria always saw as bogus.

In any case on this occasion I wanted to apologise to Gloria by sending her some flowers. As I entered the shop, a girl with white hair came up and asked if she could help me. I found her beauty astonishing. There was a sad expression in her slanted aquamarine eyes and I wondered why she looked so unhappy. I told her that I wanted to send flowers to a girl who was angry with me and I asked her what flowers she herself would like to receive from a man who was trying to make her a gesture of apology. She didn't smile. She ignored my clearly flirtatious question. She suggested I send a dozen red roses. I didn't feel this was a particuarly original or inspired choice but I agreed to her suggestion and thanked her for helping me. I asked her what her name was and she told me it was Cressida Rawlings. I asked her if she had been working in the florist's for long and she said she had started the job only a week ago. She didn't like it particularly but at least flowers were pure and she was glad to be selling them for that reason. 'Not many other things in this city seem very pure,' she said. I found this rather an eccentric remark and I asked her what she meant by it. She shrugged. Another customer had come into the shop and she went to attend to him. The florist's shop had the most marvellous smell of the intermingling scents of various flowers. I started to associate this beautiful and delicate blonde girl with the intoxicating smell of the place where she worked. When I got back to my flat I rang her up. I told her my name and explained that I was the man who had just bought the red roses. I asked her if she would like to have dinner. She sounded hesitant and suspicious. Rather to my surprise, however, she agreed to meet me that night. I offered to pick her up around eight o'clock. 'You can't come to my place,' she said. 'It's foul where I live. It's not fit for human habitation.' I told her I didn't mind. 'I mind,' she said. She asked me for my address and said she would come to my flat at whatever time suited me. I agreed to this although suddenly I wished I hadn't asked her to dine with me. Already I found her disturbingly weird.

She arrived at my flat punctually at eight. She was neatly but dowdily dressed. She was wearing make-up and she gave the impression she had rarely worn any before. She had put two hectic scarlet rounds of rouge on her cheeks and outlined her lips with greasy vermilion lipstick. She had the whorish look of a child that has painted itself in order to try to look grown up. The red make-up emphasised the excessive whiteness of her skin which had a wax-like texture, like that of lilies. Because lilies remind me of funeral services, it reminded me of death.

I took her to a Greek restaurant in Soho. She wouldn't drink anything except water. She chose to eat only the cheapest things she saw on the menu. 'Why don't you have something more exciting?' I asked her.

'I don't need excitement,' she said.

I found her very hard to talk to. She would suddenly make odd and intense remarks and there were things which she clearly felt very emotional about, but she found it hard to express them in terms that were comprehensible to anyone else. When she first arrived at my flat I saw that she was very beautiful but by the time we had finished dinner I no longer felt I could see her beauty distinctly. She made me so uncomfortable that her image already was becoming, as it was to remain for me, curiously obscured. I thought at first that she was quite intelligent but it soon became clear that she was badly educated and her outlook seemed incredibly narrow. She was incapable of discussing any general topics. She gave one the feeling she had never read a newspaper. She appeared to have no particular interests. At one point during dinner she said she believed that everyone ought to have a purpose in life. I asked her how she expected anyone to have a purpose if they didn't have a passion. 'One finds one's purpose. One makes it,' she said.

She seemed unwilling to talk about her background although I gathered her childhood had been unhappy. At one point she said she had been brought up in Devonshire. Later she contradicted herself and claimed she came from Norfolk. 'I come from a bad home. I want to forget my home and start again,' she said. Although she appeared to be totally self-involved, she lacked the ability to make her self-involvement interesting to others. She complained that the florist had only employed her because he fancied her looks. I felt this was most likely true although I couldn't see why she seemed so affronted by it. She gave me no evidence that the wretched man was importuning her in any way. She said she was miserable where she was living because the landlord owned a pass-key to her flat and as he lived in the same building, she never felt safe at night.

'Don't you have an inner bolt or chain?' I asked.

She admitted she did. Her eyes had the blank pupilless gaze that later I learned they always acquired when she was frightened.

'If a strange man has a pass-key to your flat it still doesn't exactly make you feel at ease,' she said.

By the end of dinner I found her quite tedious. She seemed extremely peculiar, but though her beauty made her seem mysterious I soon felt her peculiarities were tiresome and they ceased to have any mystery for me at all. Although this blonde girl was careful to select only the cheapest items she saw on the menu even this appeared faintly aggressive. By being so deliberately economical she removed any feeling that our dinner was an exciting occasion. I was not drinking at all heavily that night but I

57

ordered myself a bottle of wine and I noticed that she looked at each glass I poured myself with apprehension as if she feared I was about to get out of control. Even the first time we dined together, this made me get more drunk than I would have done if I had not been submitted to the worried little flicking glances that she gave me as she piously sipped her water.

That night Cressida asked me what I did. She didn't make me feel she was in the least interested but already we were starting to establish the terrible mutual politeness which was to be the keynote of our relationship. When I explained, she said she felt that to immerse oneself in the past was a waste of time — that only the future had any value. She had always hated studying history at school. 'All those nasty old wicked kings and politicians from the past, how do they affect what we do with our lives today?'

I asked her what she wanted to do with her own life — was she planning to continue to work as an assistant in the florist's shop? As she had been so dismissive about my occupation, I was anxious to point out that I was not over-impressed with hers.

'I'm going to give my life a purpose.' She spoke with great vehemence. 'I will have to make certain sacrifices to get what I want from life, but I think I've reached a point when I am prepared to make them!'

I could have asked her what sacrifices she was going to make but somehow I didn't care to know. I only wanted to pay the bill. Cressida refused to have coffee because she said it was a drug, and it had a bad effect on the liver. I was glad of this because I was longing to get away from her. The evening had been a failure. Neither of us had got any pleasure from it. I wanted to drop her home. I wondered if Gloria had received my flowers — if she would be angry if I telephoned her and asked her to join me for a late night drink.

Once we were outside the restaurant I got a taxi and asked Cressida for the address of her flat. She looked very perturbed. She turned her head and her strange aquamarine eyes gazed at me imploringly. 'Could I possibly come back to your place for a while?' she said. I asked why she wanted to do this. I tried not to make the question sound too rude. I couldn't believe she had enjoyed my company any more than I had enjoyed hers, and it puzzled me why she wanted to prolong our unsatisfactory acquaintanceship. She murmured something about her landlord having a pass-key to her flat. She said she didn't want to go back until he was asleep. She didn't like the feeling of being alone in her flat while he was still awake. None of it made much sense to me. I reminded her that she could lock her door from the inside but this didn't seem to reassure her. 'Just imagine if I was to hear him trying to turn his key in my lock. Even if he can't get in, it's the idea he may try that I find so awful. And he's such a crude beast of a man. He looks like an animal . . . You ought to see him . . .'

I asked her back for a drink. But I warned her I had to go to bed early as I had to work the following day. I was starting to dislike her. I assumed she was having an affair with her landlord. No doubt by staying out late with me she hoped to make him jealous. I suspected she was someone who complicated her life as much as possible in order to make herself more interesting.

Once she was in my flat, I felt increasingly ill at ease in her company. She sat on my sofa with her knees pressed very tightly together. She sipped a ginger ale. She reminded me of someone in a dentist's waiting room. She looked unearthly, her face was so pale except for the rounds of rouge on her cheeks which stood out like incongruous scarlet sores.

I couldn't think of anything to say to her. 'I like your flat,' she said. 'You must have a lot of money.' I grunted nervously. I found her remark gauche and embarrassing. It made her seem rather common. I excused myself and went next door to my bedroom and telephoned Gloria. I wanted to ask her to come round to have a drink once Cressida had gone. Gloria had received my roses, but they appeared to have angered rather than appeased her. She said I was trying to behave like the hero in some ancient Hollywood musical. "Wrap up some Red Roses for a Blue Lady," she hissed. 'It's too transparent and boring!'

I didn't tell her that the red roses had been Cressida's idea. I said I'd ineptly been trying to apologise for having been such bad company the previous evening. I told Gloria I'd been working on a piece which had been going very badly. I tried to explain I'd felt irritable and discouraged and that was why I'd been so inattentive and unsociable. I promised her that if she would forgive me and come round to my flat for a drink she'd find me in a much gayer and more sympathetic mood. Gloria said she had not the slightest intention of coming round. She couldn't bear the way I expected other people to submit to all the foul mood swings that depended on how my work was going. Last night she had felt she was with a monomaniac. I had bored her stiff describing my future work projects. I hadn't made Hertha Ayrton or her work on the arc lamp sound in the least engrossing as a subject, and if I ever got round to writing a book on this lady and managed to make the wretched creature and her stupid lamp seem as deadly as I had made them seem last night, she hardly felt my reputation as a biographer would prosper.

Gloria succeeded in angering me when she jeered at Hertha Ayrton. For a long time I had been obsessed by the idea of writing this woman's biography. I believed the subject to be timely because the myth that half the human race consists of 'helpless little women' with no grasp of mechanical matters still seems so firmly entrenched that it survives in every move towards equality of the sexes. Nowhere is this more true than in the engineering profession. In spite of all the official efforts to encourage women to enter engineering and technology at the moment, only 5 per cent of the girls in British universities take such courses and the woman engineer still tends to be regarded by most of her male colleagues as a strange and probably dangerous interloper. If this is the way things are now, it was a hundred times worse a century ago. Technology was then exclusively a man's world: even to be admitted to the fringes of the professions, a woman had to be superlatively brilliant, strong-willed and preferably rich. It therefore fascinated me that in spite of all these difficulties, this daughter of a Jewish clock repairer of Portsmouth managed in 1870 not only to get into the electrical engineering profession but to rise to the top of it. Her contribution to the development of the arc lamp was invaluable. She also solved formidable mathematical problems in wave theory and her scientific paper on the subject was the first paper written by a woman ever to be read at the Royal Society. Her knowledge of fluid flow was extremely important when in 1914 the poison gas attacks with phosphene and chlorine began. She designed a fan which could be used to deflect heavy poison gases away from the troops in the trenches. Over one hundred thousand Ayrton anti-gas fans were made and they saved many lives.

University education for girls was almost unknown during the nineteenth century but Hertha Ayrton was fortunate that the movement towards it had started. The educationalist Barbara Bodichon in the late 1860s succeeded in getting grudging support for setting up the first woman's college, Girton, at Cambridge University, and because her precocious gifts had attracted attention Hertha Ayrton was able to attend it. There is strong, and to me, extremely fascinating evidence that some of the money for her educational support came from George Eliot.

There is a stage when one is writing a biography when the process starts to have the childish excitement and challenge of the treasure hunt. One becomes obsessed by the pursuit of the clue. One chases these clues with frenzy into the attics of country houses, through the mouldering files of country archivists, and some of them lead only to disappointment. But one remains star-struck by the gleam of the elusive and perfect clue which can lead one to the gold of the find. When I contemplated writing a life of Hertha Ayrton, I felt one of the most enthralling pieces of detective work that confronted me would be to track down the letters which were indubitably exchanged by these two remarkable women.

I have always found it difficult to make other people share the passionate excitement I feel for any subject on which I am just about to write and with Gloria I failed abysmally. When she complained that I'd bored her by making her listen to all the reasons why I found Hertha Ayrton such an interesting figure, I was insensitive enough to try and explain and the only result was that I bored Gloria even more. I tried to tell her that the arc lamp was the dragon of the nineteenth-century electrical engineer, that its potential had fascinated and exasperated Victorian engineers since its invention by Sir Humphry Davy. Hertha Ayrton's work was extremely important for she was the first to find an explanation for the arc lamp's practical deficiencies, and therefore was able to suggest ways of eliminating them with the result that it became a reliable source of illumination which was invaluable in 1914 when there was a need for powerful search-lighting during the bombing raids by zeppelins.

None of this was in the least interesting to Gloria, who said she didn't care about the development of the arc lamp and didn't want to hear any more about it. She was no more enthusiastic when I told her that another of Hertha Ayrton's discoveries was that high speed motions in water can cause cavitation; a matter that Sir Charles Parsons found immensely significant when he came to studying high-speed propellers.

Gloria said I was being just as tedious on the subject of Hertha Ayrton's breakthroughs as I'd been last night. Nothing would induce her to come and have a drink with me. I'd already given her 'cavitation' of the brain by droning on about this tiresome woman and now she only wanted to get some sleep. I lost all sense of proportion once I started talking about my beloved project. I lost all my usual lightness of touch. I saturated people with unwanted information. And although she was glad that I planned to give my biography a feminist slant, she felt that I was a champion of woman's emancipation only in the abstract. Personal experience made her question my integrity on this particular issue. She had no doubt that intellectually I took my position seriously. But so did the left-wing radicals who love to talk about the lot of the worker as they drink champagne cocktails at the Ritz.

Gloria finished her scathing tirade by telling me she would try to read my book once I'd written it although she very much doubted she'd get through it. Meanwhile she'd prefer not to see me until my obsession with Victorian lady engineers had been worked out of my system. I felt Gloria was being vile and finally I lost my temper and slammed down the telephone. When I went back into my living room I found Cressida still sitting with her knees pressed tightly together on my sofa. She had a curious near-tearful expression on her face as if she was in the grip of some terrible panic. She looked agonised but I was feeling far too angry with Gloria to care to know why.

I slept with Cressida that night because I was feeling infuriated with Gloria. It was a very bad reason. At the time I felt I was taking some kind of revenge on Gloria for her bitchery. I was still trying to think of something devastatingly snubbing to say to her as I poured a brandy hoping to calm myself down. While I was gulping it down, the light of one of my lamps caught Cressida's lovely hair as she moved her head. Still trying to score in a fierce and imaginary argument with Gloria, I suddenly found myself stroking Cressida's silky hair. She didn't move. She froze like a rabbit caught in the dazzling headlights of a car. Then I was undoing her blouse while in my mind I continued to say insulting things to Gloria. Cressida's breasts were astonishingly white and they felt as if they were made of wax. Once again I thought of lilies, then I thought of coffins and then I thought of graves. For some reason I saw a vast field of identical white crosses. I'd once

63

seen an old photograph of the fields of the dead at Ypres.

Cressida's breathing never changed. It was unnatural. It was almost as if she wasn't breathing. As I felt up her skirt, she didn't respond. I got on top of her and she seemed so inert and delicate that I felt crass and heavy, a dead weight crushing her. She was so tight. I couldn't penetrate her. I kissed her cold white breasts and their whiteness reminded me of my laundry. I hadn't taken it to the the laundromat for a week. It wasn't natural at such a moment to be worrying about laundry. There is documented evidence that, at the age of six, Hertha Ayrton took a watch to pieces and then reassembled it. I thought about this. It wasn't natural at such a moment to be thinking about this childish feat. I suddenly wanted to stop trying to make love to this corpse-like blonde girl. Another brandy seemed more attractive than she did. I felt tired and dispirited and I would have willingly abandoned the whole doomed enterprise but Cressida's chilling silence made me too embarrassed to stop. I thought she would find it incredibly rude. 'Am I hurting you?' asked her. She didn't answer. I looked at her face. Her eyes were closed and her mouth was open and contorted in a ghastly grimace. She seemed to be in agony. Something about her tortured look exasperated me and gave me a spurt of energy. I rammed against her. Something seemed to give. I felt her tearing and Cressida gave a horrible scream. I came very quickly. I lay on top of her panting. Cressida never moved. Again I looked at her face. Her teeth were clenched. Her eyes were still closed but tears were trickling out from under her silky corn-coloured lashes. 'Thank you,' she whispered. I detested the way she thanked me. She managed to make me feel that I ought to be thanking her.

'Can I get you a taxi?' I asked her. I was being aggressive. I knew it was extremely insulting to suggest she go so soon. She hadn't even pulled down her skirt. But I knew she would refuse if I offered her a brandy and I felt soiled and disgruntled and I longed for her to go. She nodded when I offered to get her a taxi. She seemed in an odd stunned state, incapable of speaking. She reminded me of someone who has just come round from an anaesthetic at the dentist. Neither of us spoke a word until the taxi buzzed my bell. I knew it would be courteous to see her to her home but I didn't offer to do so because I hated her mournful expression. I drank half a bottle of brandy once she had left. Love never died in my marriage to Cressida. Love couldn't die. Love was never born.

After the night of our disastrous and sordid lovemaking, I did not see Cressida again for three months. I never thought about her. My affair with Gloria continued. Naturally I never told her of the episode. Gloria had an extremely jealous nature and she would not have regarded the incident as unimportant and foolish, which was the way I chose to view it. I was ashamed of my own behaviour. In retrospect I found it incomprehensible. I decided that my seduction of Cressida had been a little deranged and it was something that was best forgotten.

I was working one morning when my bell rang. A woman's voice on the buzzer system said she was Cressida Rawlings. She asked me if I remembered her. I asked her to come up to my flat, although I felt violently annoyed by the interruption as I was going through some proofs. Cressida looked very agitated as she entered. When we shook hands, I noticed again that her pupils had the disturbing habit of shrinking until she appeared to have the gaze of a blind girl.

'Are you working?' she asked me, seeing the horrible chaos of my mountainous piles of papers. 'I won't keep you,' she said.

I offered her a drink which predictably she refused. I poured myself a whisky with a martyred expression. When I'm working, I try never to drink in the daytime.

'There's something I think you should know,' Cressida said. I waited politely.

'It's not easy to explain why I've come here.' Her voice had a hysterical quaver. Deliberately I did nothing to

65

make things easy for her. My silent stare was quizzical and detached.

'I'm having your child,' she blurted.

'Nonsense!' I shouted. I was surprised by the fury of my own reaction. I slammed down my whisky glass so hard on my desk that it broke and blood spurted from my hand.

'Is your hand all right?' she asked. Her pallor was ghastly.

'No my hand isn't all right! Isn't it obvious that I've cut it? But how dare you come and disturb me when I'm working!'

'I thought you ought to know,' she said.

'I don't want to know. Why should I believe you anyway? I've only met you once. I haven't seen you for months. Then you suddenly appear and tell me you are having my child. Even if it's true that you are pregnant, why should I believe the child is mine?'

Cressida jumped as if I had struck her. Her pale dazed eyes looked deeply shocked. She didn't speak. It was as if she couldn't think of anything to say. I remember looking out of the window of my flat and noticing how dull and oppressive the sky was. There were no clouds. It was one great expanse of unbroken grey.

'You'd better have an abortion,' I said. I bandaged my bleeding hand with a handkerchief. Again she jumped as if I'd hit her.

'Oh no!' She sucked in the words with a sort of hiss.

'It's the only sensible thing for you to do.'

'Never!' she said. I saw her pupils shrinking. Her mouth twitched. I realised she was enraged but I didn't care.

'You can't expect any help from me,' I said. 'I don't want to have a child, even if it is my child.'

'It's *my* child. Never forget that!' She looked suddenly extremely malevolent, like a spitting angry cat. Cressida rarely showed anger but she showed it to me then.

'You can't make me destroy my child!' she said.

'I can't make you do anything,' I answered. 'But I'd

like you to go now. You'd better work out this depressing mess yourself. It's your fault . . . I don't want to know anything about it. So for God's sake don't come round bothering me.'

She left then with outraged silent dignity. I was just as angry as she was. I hadn't been polite. I hadn't tried to be sympathetic. I felt no remorse. In order to forget Cressida's distasteful and disruptive visit, I buried myself in my proofs. My hand kept bleeding. I hated Cressida when I saw drops of blood making disgusting messy spots on the whiteness of the page.

I never told Gloria about Cressida's visit. I suppose from the start there was something wrong with our relationship, for I always wanted to conceal important things from her. I didn't want her to become involved in my dilemma. I immersed myself in my work and rarely gave a thought to Cressida. Locked up in my study, I had the illusion that Cressida couldn't find me and I could convince myself that this creepy white-skinned girl and her distasteful pregnancy would go away.

She didn't go away. Subconsciously I must have felt some anxiety about her. I heard nothing from Cressida for about three months and one day, feeling exhausted after having worked hard all morning, I took a walk to refresh myself and I found that I was passing the florist's shop where I had originally met her. Something compelled me to go in to see if she was still working there.

It was a shock seeing her. She was mixing carnations with feathery green fern and wrapping them up in tissue paper. When she saw me her aquamarine eyes looked at me so blankly that I wasn't quite sure if she remembered who I was.

'How are you?' I said.

'I'm very well.' Politeness was starting to grip us in the way that hoar frost can grip mud and turn it as hard as rock.

She was very pregnant. To me she looked obscenely pregnant. Her frail body looked incongruous carrying such

67

an immensely protruding abdomen. Her swollen belly seemed like a malignant growth. Her face was whiter than ever. It was also much thinner. She had dark panda-like smudges under her eyes. She looked extremely unwell.

'So you decided to have it,' I said.

Her eyes suddenly flashed with crazy defiance.

'Naturally,' she snapped. 'No one can stop me!'

'I imagine it's much too late for that now.' I stared despondently at her stomach.

'I am very happy,' she said aggressively.

'When is it coming?' I asked.

'In three months.'

'Can you manage?'

'I'll have to.' Our dialogue was deadly.

'Where are you going to live?'

'I don't know.'

'Do you still have the same flat?'

'For the moment. But I can't stay on there. My land-lord won't allow dogs or children.'

'Where will you go?'

'I don't know.' Her aggressive attitude suddenly vanished and for a second she looked quite desperate.

'Will you go on working here?'

'I won't be able to. They don't want a child here. And I'm not putting any child of mine in a day care centre!'

'I have to go,' I said. I found it intolerable to stay with her for one more second.

'I'll come and see you again,' I said. 'Maybe I can think of something to do to help you.'

Cressida shrugged hopelessly. She had the face of a miserable child.

I didn't marry Cressida out of kindness. It would be more honest to say that I married her out of convention-ality. I believed it would be incorrect not to marry her.

I had various reactions in the weeks that followed my visit to the florist's shop. I felt an immense anger. I had the suspicion that she had intended to become pregnant and had come to my flat for that purpose. The way she had covered her face with such an excessive amount of make-up on that particular evening seemed extremely suspicious. She had used me as a stud and the tactics by which she had tricked me seemed cold-blooded and they enraged me. I detested this near-albino girl for making me feel that I ought to do something to help her. I couldn't forgive her for having deliberately contrived to get herself into a situation where she could exert her pernicious emotional blackmail. Although I had moods in which I tried to convince myself that she was lying when she claimed that I was the father of her unborn child, I had the horrible suspicion that it was true. Her look of shock when I said that I doubted that she was pregnant by me had seemed too genuine. There was no question she was still a virgin when I slept with her, and she seemed so sexless that I rather doubted she had slept with anyone else subsequently. But I had no way of being certain.

If I accepted that she was having my child, I still found it deeply unacceptable that I had no control at all as to whether it should be born or not. The idea of this child was repugnant to me. I saw it as the child of lovelessness and sordor. The prospect of its birth filled me with apprehension and gloom.

In certain moods I decided to ignore Cressida's plight. I felt she deserved to suffer the consequences of her own wilfulness. If she had a difficult time raising her child alone with nowhere to live and no means of support, it was her own decision that had placed her in such an un-enviable situation. She was responsible for the way that she wanted to live her life and I saw no reason why I should have to worry about her future. I kept reminding myself that I hardly knew her.

Just when I had decided that I would be ruthless and refuse to let her involve me in her odious pregnancy, I remembered her look of desperation in the florist's shop. I remembered how vulnerable and frail she looked. As I said before, conventionality rather than kindness made me feel it was incorrect to do nothing to help a homeless pregnant girl when I had been partially instrumental in creating the unpromising situation in which she now found herself.

When I decided to go to the florist's and tell her that I would marry her, my motives were selfish as well as chivalrous. If I married her I felt I could forget her and she would cease to haunt me and prevent me from concentrating on my work. Marriage has never seemed a sacred institution to me. I hoped I could marry her, give her a name for her child, find her somewhere to live, and then if needs be, divorce her. A marriage licence was only a piece of paper. I couldn't believe that my life need be changed by a legal form.

When I told Cressida I was prepared to marry her, I did it quite brutally. She was still working in the florist's. She was much more pregnant and looking even more desperate and ill. I still remember the smell of flowers while I was talking to her. I no longer found them intoxicating and marvellous. They seemed to smell of poison that morning. I felt allergic to them. I told Cressida that if we married, I would consider the marriage to be nothing more than a technicality. I was prepared to support her but I didn't want to live in the same house or see her very often. She must make her own life and bring up the child without making many demands on me. I would always consider the child to be hers rather than mine and she must never expect me to love it.

Cressida listened to all this in silence. She didn't seem any more enthusiastic about our prospective marriage than I was. In fact she had such a dubious anxious expression that I wondered if she was considering turning my lukewarm proposal down. Then she sighed and she seemed to reconsider my offer.

'I suppose it would be best for the child,' she said. 'It would have a name. I suppose that's important.' Her face then brightened and she suddenly gave a triumphant little smile as she added, 'And anyway, the child will always have me.'

We married the following week in a register office. I never told Gloria that I had married. I dined with her the day of my marriage and never mentioned it. I never told my parents or any of my friends. By not mentioning it, I tried to deny that it had really happened.

A few months after the birth of Mary Rose, I told Gloria that I had a wife and a child who were living in the country. Understandably she was outraged that I hadn't informed her before. I was unable to think up any satisfactory excuse to explain my peculiar reticence on this matter. When I made my shock announcement, Gloria threw a hysterical sobbing fit and called me a bigamist. Feeling defensive, because I knew that Gloria had every right to be incensed by my duplicity, I reminded her that I had never asked her to be my wife and was never going to do so. This did little to soothe Gloria's wounded feelings. I did not tell her how recently I had married. I thought she might have a nervous breakdown if she was told the truth. I pretended that I had been married to Cressida for several years. I also lied about Mary Rose's age. I made out that she was two years older than she was.

The awful day that we married, Cressida and I hardly spoke a word to each other before the ceremony. We got a couple of strangers from the streets to be our witnesses. The registrar conducted the ceremony in an embarrassingly ecclesiastical fashion. He might have been a bishop preaching in a cathedral. It was as if he was vainly striving to give the occasion a little solemnity. There were chrysanthemums on his desk, which he treated like an altar. As we exchanged our vows, I was all the time aware of these depressing autumn flowers. They looked sad and wilted, and their petals were soggy and brown.

Once it was over, Cressida and I thanked each other for coming. At that point our mutual politeness was so excessive, it became grotesque. I dropped her back to the florist's and returned to my flat to work. I didn't see Cressida again until she was in the hospital where our ill-fated child was born.

71

Chapter Five

'Is anything the matter, dearest?' I called out to my wife the night that I heard her nervously tapping on my door. My tone was casual and avuncular. I behaved as if I found it normal that she should have come to wake me. The door opened. Cressida remained standing on the threshold as if unwilling to enter. She was wearing a ludicrously old-fashioned flannel nightgown which matched the whiteness of her face. It was primly buttoned at the neck with small pearl buttons. I found something disturbing about her nightdress. It was that of a small Victorian girl.

Cressida was wearing her tow-coloured hair loose in a way she had not worn it for years. As she stood there with her bare feet in a pigeon-toed position she looked both childish and like a woman who was masquerading in order to look younger, which made her appear oddly old.

'That child still hasn't turned up,' she said.

'It's only been missing for twenty-four hours. That's not very long.' I pulled the patchwork quilt up to my chin. I felt uneasy talking to my wife from my bed.

'I haven't slept at all,' Cressida said.

'I'm so sorry. I wish I had a sleeping pill that I could give you.'

'I don't want a sleeping pill,' she spoke very sharply, as if my suggestion had angered her. 'The last thing I want is to be drugged. I want to have my wits about me on a night like this.'

'Why don't you make yourself a cup of tea? Maybe that will help you get to sleep.' Everything I suggested sounded inadequate. My wife seemed to be in an acutely anxious state. She kept rolling her eyes towards the small latticed window in my bedroom as if she feared someone was about to enter it. She kept cocking her head and listening as if she was trying to hear something outside in the garden.

'I didn't lock the back door!' she said. There was something accusatory in the way she told me this. It was certainly most unlike her to forget to lock up the cottage. She was usually scrupulous about security and if she had retired before I got back from the pub she always got up after I returned and went downstairs to see that the doors and windows were closed.

'I shouldn't worry about the back door,' I said. 'I very much doubt we'll have a burglary tonight.'

'I can't sleep knowing that the door is open.' Her voice had a quavering desperation.

I found her behaviour baffling. I couldn't understand why she had come into my bedroom and woken me. If she couldn't sleep while the back door was open, why didn't she simply go downstairs and lock it so that her mind could be at ease?

'I didn't dare to go near the door.' Her voice was still choked and she seemed to be on the verge of tears. Her tension filled the little guest room and I experienced it as electric. I felt it could set fire to the black Elizabethan beam.

'Why were you frightened to go near the back door?' I asked.

'I felt something was out there behind it.'

'Oh really, Cressida,' I said, 'that really is nonsense.' Cressida had lived in Beckham for the last six years and she had never once complained she felt frightened to be in the cottage alone. And this was one of the rare occasions when she had a man in the house.

'You couldn't go down and lock the back door?' she asked. I could tell that she found it painful to have to appeal to me. It was almost unheard of for her to make any direct demands.

'I'll go and lock it of course, dearest,' I said in a tone that was mildly martyred.

'Something ghastly has happened in this village,' my wife said as if to explain her irrational behaviour. 'And something worse is about to happen. I can feel these things . . .' And standing there in her absurd flannel nightdress with her hair dishevelled and her pale eyes swivelling, she reminded me of a crazed Cassandra.

'Why don't you go back to your bedroom and calm yourself down?' I said. 'I'll go down and lock the door and then you've really got to stop worrying. Nothing particularly ghastly has happened. Or at least nothing that I'm aware of. You are over-tired and over-excited . . .'

I didn't want to get out of bed until I had persuaded her to leave the guest room. I couldn't bear her to see me in my pyjamas. Cressida had already violated one of the most important principles by which we sustained our marriage when she entered my bedroom wearing only her nightgown. This suggested she was in a most unusual state of mind and I wanted our habitual formality restored immediately.

'I'll go down and lock the door if you will just go back to your bedroom,' I kept assuring her.

'Thank you,' she said as she left. She spoke with exaggerated intensity and her gratitude seemed much too felt. It made me extremely uneasy.

I got up and put on a dressing gown and went down the ladder staircase. The cottage was so silent that every step I took made the beams and timbers creak and moan. I went to the back door which was near the larder. I saw that it was ajar. It was completely dark outside in the garden. It was unpleasantly still and there was no moon. Just for a moment I felt an absurd sensation of panic as if I had been infected by Cressida's hysteria. Could there really be someone lurking outside that door? I flung it open in order to reassure myself that my fears were groundless. I then stepped out into the garden and peered

74

into the darkness. There was not a sound out there. But somehow I didn't like the silence. The hush filled me with foreboding. I longed for some cock to crow, for some far-off dog to bark. I went back into the cottage and bolted the door. There was only one lamp turned on in the living room and it didn't give as much light as I would have liked. I went creaking back up the ladder staircase and along the little landing that led to the bedroom my wife shared with Mary Rose. I knocked softly on her door. I wanted to tell her the cottage was locked up. She didn't answer. I found that strange for I very much doubted she was asleep, but I didn't like to knock any louder for I knew it would enrage her if I woke the child. I went back to the poky little guest room feeling extremely glad that in the morning I was going to tell her I wanted a divorce.

In the morning I felt much better. It was a relief not to have a searing hangover. Cressida was downstairs. I could hear the sound of her radio rising from the kitchen. Once I had dressed and shaved I went down to join her. I planned to discuss the divorce once Mary Rose had gone to school.

When I came into the kitchen, I found my wife sitting by the table with its gay red and white check cloth. She had the radio on her knee and she was nursing it like a baby. She looked awful. Her face was haggard and her pallor had a greenish hue. Her eyes were swollen as if she'd spent the whole night crying. Her hair was still loose but she hadn't remembered to brush it. It was ridiculous; she seemed a wreck. A child whose name she had only heard on the television was missing.

'Good morning, dearest.' I greeted my wife with my customary jaunty politeness. For once she didn't bother to answer, nor did she go scurrying around like a humble skivvy fetching me my breakfast. She remained in a desolate frozen position by the table. Her head was bowed in order to hear the radio.

'They still haven't found her,' she said.

'It's only about twenty-four hours that she's been

missing. That's not very long,' I said.

'It's much more than that,' Cressida said, 'she's not been heard of since the night before last.'

Cressida usually made me proper coffee for she knew I hated the synthetic taste of instant. This morning she hadn't bothered to make me any. I made a cup for myself while she remained miserably cradling the radio.

I noticed that she hadn't even taken the trouble to make any breakfast for Mary Rose. My daughter should have been glad of this but nothing seemed to make her glad. She sat beside her mother looking more subdued and unhealthy than usual. She stared fretfully at the kitchen stove and the sight of it seemed to make her feel intensely sad.

'I've got to get back to London very soon,' I said.

Cressida didn't answer. She kept switching the knob of the radio hoping to get the latest news. She found a programme on which an irritatingly bland housewife was reciting some recipe for a homemade pie.

'Do we have to have that so loud, dearest?' I asked her. My wife turned the volume louder and her pale eyes stared aggressively at me.

'You don't care at all, do you?'

'Care about what? Care about homemade pies?'

'You don't care that they can't find that child.'

'Of course I care.' I was lying. 'But I don't know the child. If it's missing there's precious little I can do to find it. I have to confess I feel somewhat removed from the whole business.'

'I don't feel removed,' Cressida said.

'It's different for you,' I said. 'You are a mother.'

'You are a father, aren't you?'

We were getting nowhere. I looked at my watch. I wondered when Mary Rose would be taken to school. I wanted to talk to my wife about the divorce.

'Did you know it's already ten o'clock?' I asked her. 'Isn't Mary Rose going to be late for school?'

'Mary Rose isn't going to school.'

'Why not?' A peculiar expression came over my wife's face. For a moment she looked witch-like. It was as if she had aged about twenty years in the night.

'Mary Rose has a cold.'

'Does she? I'm sorry.' I examined my daughter, who was still mesmerised by Cressida's gas stove. Even when the child was talked about, she never registered that she was aware of it. She lived in her own world but her disconsolate expression gave no sign it was a world that any one could envy. I saw no evidence that she was suffering from a cold. But then to me Mary Rose always looked pasty and out of sorts. Her breathing was always adenoidal so that she gave the impression that she was afflicted by a permanent cold.

'Does she have a temperature?'

Cressida didn't answer. She had found the news on her radio. She listened impatiently to reports of the oil crisis and various international political upheavals. Finally the newscaster said the Kent police were making further inquiries into the disappearance of Maureen Sutton from Beckham.

'You see?' Cressida said to me.

'See what?'

'They haven't found her.'

'It's starting to get worrying,' I agreed. I was more worried by the fact that it seemed the wrong moment to tell my wife that I wanted a divorce.

I went out of the back door into the garden. Cressida's cottage seemed particularly suffocating to me that morning. I needed to get some air before I could decide what I was going to do.

Our garden was little more than a back yard. It was drab and unremarkable. I couldn't understand why I'd found it menacing the night before. Cressida kept it tidy but she gave it none of the frenetic love and attention that she lavished on the cottage. A few dusty-looking primulas had been planted in its meagre flower beds. Its patio of crazy-paving stones had been weeded, but beyond that our garden had nothing more than a patch of mown grass on which there was a slide which was never used by Mary Rose.

Mrs Butterhorn was leaning over the fence when I came out to get some air. She was our closest neighbour. Her house and her garden directly adjoined Cressida's cottage.

Mrs Butterhorn was a woman who took a pride in the fact that she had 'let herself go'. She gloried in the horror of her appearance because for her it symbolised the emancipation that had come to her late in life. Mrs Butterhorn was the widow of a wealthy London stockbroker who had died a couple of years before. She had used the money he had left her to buy a house in Beckham and now she devoted her life to the only thing she loved, her beautiful garden.

'One thing I'll say for my poor old dear departed,' Mrs Butterhorn often boomed at me. 'He deprived me of everything I found worth living for while he was on this earth. But he paid me back in death because now I'm starting life again and I'm as free as a bird!'

Mrs Butterhorn looked more manly than most men. She was short and extremely stout. Her body was almost entirely square. She was usually dressed in khaki for she bought most of her clothes from an army surplus store. She never spoke, she only boomed in a raucous upper class accent. When one heard her bellowing orders to her ancient arthritic gardener, one knew one was listening to 'the voice that was born to command'.

Although Mrs Butterhorn claimed that she liked to 'keep herself to herself', she was in fact an incurable busybody. She had a belligerent curiosity about all the other inhabitants of Beckham and my wife and I particularly intrigued her because although she spied on us continually, our marriage continued to mystify her.

Mrs Butterhorn frequented the Red Lion in the evenings and I dreaded it whenever she managed to trap me in some smoky corner. 'I'm afraid I look a perfect fright today,' she would say triumphantly in order to open a conversation. I wished that she wasn't proud of it. She was always filthy dirty and her clothes smelt of manure. Her broken nails were invariably clogged with mud. She clumped around in unwashed wellingtons. Her cropped steel-grey hair stuck up in uneven tufts as if it had been chopped off with gardening shears. She deliberately cultivated an eccentric appearance because she liked the idea of being known as 'a character' in Beckham. Her dream was to be like an unusual landmark that could be pointed out to visitors in the way they were shown the oast-house and Beckham's antique well.

'I toed the line when I was married to Mervyn,' she told me. 'I ran Mervyn's house in Mayfair and I entertained his business contacts. I let him trap me in that filthy sink of a city. My life was one long round of gentility and graciousness and endless sherry parties. I dressed myself up in all the right little grey silk dresses. I was the perfect ladylike wife with blue-rinsed curls and rows of expensive pearls! But now with Mervyn's death all that's behind me . . . Now you'll find me where I've always longed to be – out in the open all day. At last I can work with the soil, which is the only thing I've ever loved. Mervyn always detested being in the country. Mervyn was a city man. He was fond of his club and he was fond of his office. He was the sort of man who was frightened of cows and summer flowers upset him because they gave him hay fever.'

I found Mrs Butterhorn exhausting when she described her ill-matched marriage to Mervyn. In the past she had occasionally invited me to have a drink in her house and I had accepted because I could think of no polite way to refuse. Her house was much larger than Cressida's cottage. It had been built at the same time and had similar uneven floors and latticed windows and its ceilings slanted with massive black Tudor beams. With evident relish Mrs Butterhorn maintained her house in a state of filth and chaos. She had dirty dishes littered all over the furniture in her living room. She boasted that she now ate and drank whenever she felt like it and no longer needed to subject herself to the tyranny of regular meals.

'I often make myself steak and onions at six in the morning,' she told me. 'And I wash it down with a bottle of the finest Courvoisier brandy!' I disliked seeing traces of these irregular meals all over her house. There were empty brandy bottles everywhere and they were filled with cigarette stubs because she used them as ash trays. She kept several cats and dogs and they had ripped her sofas and chairs, which were stained and smelly and covered with animal hair. If you picked up a cup or a glass in Mrs Butterhorn's house you feared you were going to stick to it. She had spades and hoes and pails and other gardening equipment scattered in piles all over her threadbare carpets, for she used her living room as a tool shed. Sometimes when I went from the astringent cleanliness of my wife's cottage to the rebelliously arranged dirt and confusion of Mrs Butterhorn's establishment, I expected to feel a sense of relief. But I never found the experience as agreeable as I expected. With my aversion to cats I felt sickened by the way that her house always stank of cats' urine. Mrs Butterhorn's belief that by flouting all standards of basic hygiene she was leading a pioneering life of purity and beauty was a notion I was too squeamish and conventional to share.

If one stepped out of Mrs Butterhorn's house and went into her garden, however, the transition was overwhelming. It was like stepping from Hell direct into Paradise. I know very little about gardening but whenever I saw what she had done with it, I recognised it was some kind of work of genius. Whereas almost everything in her house was damaged and evil-smelling, everything in her garden was lovingly tended and perfect. Her garden was much the largest in Beckham and it was unrivalled in its beauty. Mrs Butterhorn spent every minute of the day working with her ancient gardener to improve it. She was out there even in the foulest weather pruning, weeding, transplanting, spraying and tying plants up with wire. Sometimes late at night I looked out of the guest room window and I'd see Mrs Butterhorn still toiling frenetically, using the light of an old oil lamp. I found Mrs Butterhorn an inquisitive old bore but when she showed me her garden, I always felt an unwilling respect for her. However incredible it looked with its subtly beautiful profusion of exotic plants and flowers, she never seemed to be in the least pleased with it as it was. She only talked of how she hoped it would look when some newly sown seed eventually came up, when some problematic plant started to bud. Her attitude towards the lovely garden she had created was so modest and dissatisfied that it gave her a dignity and pathos. It made me feel she was an artist, for it seemed her garden was only able to bloom for her in some teasingly unobtainable future.

The morning I wanted to talk to my wife about a divorce, I was not at all pleased to see Mrs Butterhorn's face coming over the fence. She was obviously in a gregarious mood.

'Isn't it dreadful about that child?' she said.

'What child?' I asked. I felt the missing child had already over-run my wife's cottage. It depressed me to find that like a fast-spreading weed she was now taking over my back yard.

'That local child that's disappeared. It's causing quite a stir. They've reported it on the radio. And I saw it all over the television last night.'

I shrugged and lit a cigarette.

'Those women on the council estate take so little care of their children, it's surprising more of them don't disappear.'

I shrugged again without answering her.

'They let their children run wild. They never bother to get them in at night. A lot of those council estate women are no better than animals. They shouldn't be allowed to be mothers. They have no sense of responsibility . . .'

I would have liked to have said something crushing to Mrs Butterhorn but I knew from experience that she held very definite views on a variety of subjects and any attempt to squash them was a total waste of time.

'When a child disappears in a small community, it's never very pleasant,' she continued. 'It makes you start thinking. It reminds you of all the horrific things you have read about in the papers. If a child suddenly vanishes from a deprived area like the council estate it's not likely to be kidnapping.'

'Surely no one has ever suggested that there's been a kidnapping,' I said irritably. 'The child may have had an accident. A million things may have happened to her.'

I felt that Mrs Butterhorn was being as tiresome as my wife. They were both starved of drama and anxious to whip up a spurious excitement about every local mishap.

Mrs Butterhorn's bulging toad-like eyes examined me with a pitying expression.

'You men never like to face up to the uglier possibilities of life,' she said. 'Mervyn was like that too. Mervyn was a great escapist. His head was always buried in the sand.'

I very much disliked being compared to Mervyn. I had formed the most unfavourable mental picture of the man. Mrs Butterhorn continued remorselessly with her perfidious comparison.

'Mervyn's attitude would have been exactly the same as yours if he'd been told a child was missing. "I'm sure that child is all right," Mervyn would have said. "Why jump to conclusions?" '

'There isn't much point in jumping to dire conclusions,' I said dryly.

'That's always the man's attitude.' Mrs Butterhorn nodded her head knowingly. 'Men have no sense of the dangers that are always lurking round the corner. Women face up to these things much more. They have twice the imagination . . .'

I only wished she would stop talking so I had some peace to plan the best way to approach Cressida about a divorce.

'Now your wife must be very upset about the disappearance of this child,' Mrs Butterhorn continued insistently. 'It can't make her feel very comfortable. If I had a small girl of my own this would make me very nervous. And your wife is such a devoted mother. Believe me, it's rare to see such devotion in this day and age. Most of the young women nowadays are too selfish to give much time to their youngsters. But your wife is very special and sometimes I can't help thinking her life can't be exactly easy. As her neighbour I can't help noticing that she is alone a lot. I don't want to be impertinent but I sometimes wonder if she gets quite the support from you that she's entitled to. I know you are a busy man and your work detains you in London, but isn't there some way that you could arrange to be down here with your family more often? I'm sure your little daughter must suffer from your long absences. Sometimes I see your wife trudging home from school with the child and my heart goes out to both of them . . . They look so downcast. After all your wife is a very beautiful young woman and for months she leads the life of a hermit . . . But I hope you don't think I'm being interfering saying all this.'

I decided to go back into the cottage. The last thing I wanted at that moment was to receive marriage bureau-type advice from Mrs Butterhorn.

'As I've said, your wife is an excellent mother,' she continued. 'I take my hat off to her. If I were to make a criticism I'd say she keeps your daughter at home too much. She doesn't let her mix with other children. I've never once seen her invite any of your daughter's school friends to tea. And children need company of their own age. It's immensely important to their development.'

'If you'll excuse me,' I said. 'I'm driving up to London this morning and I have several things to attend to.'

When I went back inside the cottage I noticed Cressida hadn't moved from the kitchen table where she was sitting, still hugging the radio.

'The police are extending their inquiries,' she said.

'That's good,' I answered.

83

'I don't see that it's good at all. I think the whole thing is starting to look extremely serious.'

I suddenly longed to be back in my London flat where I could work on my life of Hertha Ayrton. I felt it would be unwise to raise the subject of divorce at a moment when my wife was already so upset. I decided I could talk to her about it on the telephone during the week, or if that seemed too heartless I could come down the following Saturday and discuss the matter with her then.

'I must be going,' I said. I went over and awkwardly kissed my daughter on her forehead. She hardly seemed to notice my kiss. She continued to stare blankly in front of her. Her forehead felt icy cold. When I drove away from the cottage, Cressida always made her wave goodbye. But that day when I left for London, my departure went unnoticed by my wife and child.

Chapter Six

I always felt exhilarated driving back to London after leaving Cressida's cottage and that particular morning I was even more elated than usual. As I drove through the drab sprawl of the suburbs I noticed only the daffodils planted in the window boxes of the grimy little houses.

Once Cressida and I had started divorce proceedings I resolved to have no further contact with her. I was prepared to make her a settlement but after that I was determined never again to be made to feel it was my duty to visit the cottage. It now seemed to me that my reasons for making all the agonising visits that I'd paid my family in the past had been neurotic rather than benevolent and honourable. It was as if from time to time I'd needed reassuring evidence that Cressida and Mary Rose were still alive, that they had not perished from the lack of affection I felt for them.

I doubted Cressida would make extortionate demands on me if I asked her for a divorce. She took immense pride in her excessive frugality and always tried to make me look at her household accounts when I came down to the cottage. But her thrift brought me little joy. In fact I often saw it as pathological. I was not grateful for the fact that she never presented me with laundry bills. It made me uneasy and ill-tempered when I saw her going off to the woods with a hatchet like some early American settler to chop her own logs. I suspected that it was guilt that made her so economical. She had forced me to take financial responsibility for her country ménage and she assuaged her conscience by claiming that she and the child cost me virtually nothing. It suited her to believe this. But however Cressida slaved and stinted, she never convinced me it was true.

When I got back to my flat that day, I telephoned Gloria and asked her to dine with me. She asked me sarcastically if I'd enjoyed my weekend. I said that it had been uneventful.

I decided not to tell Gloria that I had finally made up my mind to divorce Cressida. I was frightened she would be over-interested by this information.

We met that evening in a restaurant in Soho. Gloria was wearing a slinky black dress and was looking elegant and lovely. She sometimes startled me by the way she managed to look exactly like those haughty high fashion models who advertise expensive products in glossy magazines. Her appearance urged one to drink ice-cold Martinis that were carried in on salvers by silver-haired old butlers, to smoke Turkish cigarettes in the flickering candlelight of chandeliers. By subliminal rather than overt means Gloria's appearance promised one sex. Never humdrum everyday sex but some kind of physical encounter that was exquisite and recherché and associated with yachts and ancient castles and very far from the experience of the common man.

Before I ordered any drinks, I asked her if she could refrain from making any jibing references to my wife, as I hoped that we would get through the evening without quarrelling. Gloria said that she hadn't the slightest intention of mentioning my wife, that she found my marriage to pathetic it was not worth talking about. For once I refused to rise.

'A child is missing from the village where your wife lives,' Gloria said.

'How do you know?' It shocked me to be told this by Gloria.

'I heard it on the television.'

'I expect she will soon be found.' I poured myself some wine.

'My God, you do have an unpleasant attitude to things!' Gloria said.

'What attitude ought I to take?'

'You needn't be so bland and smug! A little girl vanishes and the police give out an announcement that they suspect foul play. How can you be so callous? How can you blithely sit there telling me you are sure she'll soon be found?'

'Foul play?' I asked her sharply. 'How do you know they suspect foul play?'

'They announced that on the television too. How do you think I know? I don't live in Beckham, fortunately.'

'Did you hear anything else about it on the news?'

'They showed a picture of the child. She had an adorable little face. The whole thing is horrible really . . .'

I banged my fist on the table.

'Oh, for God's sake, Gloria, don't *you* start weeping about that child!'

'What on earth is the matter with you?' Gloria's dark eyes stared at me in amazement. I wasn't certain myself why I'd reacted quite so violently. I longed to make Gloria stop talking about that missing child, although I realised this was unreasonable. She had a perfect right to discuss it if she chose to. Yet the subject was extremely distasteful to me. First my wife, then Mrs Butterhorn and now Gloria, they all seemed to enjoy morbidly speculating on the fate of this small girl. I disliked the way they spoke about her in hushed and reverential tones as if she was dead. There was not a scrap of evidence that she was dead . . .

'I saw the child's mother on the television,' Gloria said. 'The poor woman broke down in front of the cameras. It was ghastly. It was one of those things you wish you'd never seen. I don't think they should be allowed to televise people in moments of tragedy. It's barbaric . . .'

'Why did she go on television?'

'She was making an appeal. If anyone saw her little girl

last Saturday evening, she wants them to go to the police.'

'I see.' Realising my response must seem inadequate I tried to improve it by adding ponderously, 'Beckham is a very small village so I imagine someone will have seen her.'

After that we were both silent and our silence was not a comfortable one.

'I'm glad I'm not your wife,' Gloria murmured reflectively after we'd sat staring at each other for some time.

'I asked you not to discuss my wife!' I flared up immediately.

'Don't be so absurd and bellingerent. I haven't the faintest desire to talk about your wife. I'm just saying that I'm glad I'm not her. I certainly wouldn't like to be alone with a child in that village tonight. I shouldn't imagine any woman in Beckham will sleep very well.'

I remembered Cressida's eccentric behaviour when she came into the guest room, her peculiar fear of going down to lock the back door. What was she doing tonight? Was she sitting up sleepless with Mary Rose listening for noises in the back yard? I decided there was no point worrying about it. If Cressida chose to work herself into a state of foolish panic it was not my problem. It was ironic that just when I had finally decided that I'd cease to make any pretence of concerning myself with Cressida's welfare, Gloria seemed to feel I should have remained in Beckham in order to keep her company and allay her fears.

'Is the cottage where your wife lives very isolated?' Gloria asked me.

'Not particularly. In fact there is an elderly woman who lives in a house right next door to her.'

'Is there a man in that house?'

'No, there isn't. The woman is a widow and lives alone.'

'If I was your wife I wouldn't feel an old woman was much protection.'

'Protection against what, for God's sake?' Gloria was now really starting to annoy me.

Gloria shrugged her shoulders and gave me a pitying look as if to say that time would tell.

Chapter Seven

The next day I worked from eight in the morning until about three in the afternoon. Gloria left my flat early to do an interview with some American actress who was staying at the Dorchester. I took my telephone off the hook and spoke to no one all day. When I finally stopped working, I made myself some coffee and took a bath. I decided to telephone Cressida and tell her that I wanted to come down to Beckham next Saturday in order to talk about our future. I thought it was important to warn her there was a special purpose to this visit.

'The police are going to do a massive search of the woods behind the council estate!' Cressida sounded extremely agitated.

'So that child still hasn't been found.'

'If she'd been found the police would hardly be planning to search the woods for her.'

'That's true,' I said lamely.

'You know they suspect foul play?' Cressida's voice was husky and choked.

'I know. Someone told me.'

'She was only a few months older than Mary Rose.'

'Cressida,' I interrupted, 'I'm coming down to Beckham on Saturday. There are serious things we ought to discuss.'

'Did you see that child's mother on the television?'

'No.'

'The father was on television too. They seemed to be the most devoted couple. I couldn't bear to see the frightful state they were in. They were quite young. She was their only child. They both looked destroyed. The poor woman was crying so much she could hardly speak. Mary Rose and I prayed for the Suttons most of the night.'

My only reaction was a feeling of nausea. Cressida was religious and I therefore accepted that she'd find it natural to pray for this unknown couple. But to make Mary Rose pray with her . . . I imagined my daughter kneeling puppet-like beside her mother with her emaciated little fingers pressed piously together as she uncomprehendingly repeated the prayers that Cressida fed her.

'The police are making inquiries all over the village,' my wife continued. I felt defeated and for a moment I was tempted to abandon the idea of asking her for a divorce. Why not leave things as they were? Our marriage was so meaningless there seemed no particular urgency to dissolve it. If I ceased to visit Cressida, our polite and unenviable relationship would end automatically. Yet I still believed that for me it was symbolically important that I divorce her. Once I was legally free, I hoped no longer to be plagued by any guilty feeling that it was my responsibility to keep seeing this lonely little couple in Kent.

I repeated that I wanted to come down at the weekend to talk about our future. Cressida showed no interest at all. She went on as before talking in a hectic way about little Maureen Sutton. As she usually disliked speaking on the telephone her garrulousness was disquieting. I was extremely glad when I finally managed to interrupt her overwrought stream of talk in order to say goodbye.

Gloria came round to my flat just before dinner. She was in an exultant mood, saying she was pleased with the interview she had done with the American actress. As far as I could make out, this woman had given Gloria a long list of her past Broadway and off-Broadway triumphs followed by another long list of all the stage and film roles she was currently considering. Gloria asked me if I would read her article once she had got it typed. She must have sensed my lack of eagerness although I told her I would love to see it.

'I think you might sound more enthusiastic!'

'To be frank, Gloria, I'm sure your interview is very well done. But I've never heard of this actress. I don't especially care to know what plays or musical hits she's been in. I have no interest in hearing about her divorces. I don't wish to know what she thinks about men. In fact I must admit that as a subject this woman doesn't interest me enormously.'

'Angela Cleveland is an immensely talented woman. I think it's disgustingly snobbish the way you never want to know about anyone who has had a popular success. You're probably jealous, if the truth be known.'

'Look, I never go to musical comedies as you know. I don't particularly like the modern theatre. So I have very little curiosity about show biz personalities. That's all there is to it.'

'I still find your attitude insufferably superior. The woman I interviewed today was a brilliant and fascinating creature. I hope that some of her charm and humour will come through in my article. I found it quite a difficult and challenging piece to write. I don't see why you have to be so patronising about it.'

'Type it out and let me read it,' I said. 'I obviously can't judge something I haven't seen.'

Gloria tapped the ash off her cigarette with a petulant gesture. 'I don't feel like showing it to you,' she said. 'I know how sarcastic you will be. You try to discourage everything I do. You may not feel that Angela Cleveland is an interesting person to write about, but don't forget that many people may find that Hertha Ayrton is also a subject of quite limited appeal.'

We were sparring once again. We were infantile. Gloria and I used the most trivial issues to start bonfires. After we'd struck our matches, we used any old twig or ball of paper to create a blaze.

Gloria flounced across the room and turned on the

television much too loud. She often did this when I had annoyed her because she knew the sound was excruciatingly painful to me. I thought of going over to turn the volume down but realised that she wanted our dispute to degenerate into a physical battle with curses, slaps and tears. I went into my bedroom and shut the door in order to muffle the hateful noise of the television. I lay on my bed and started to read. If I ignored Gloria's attempts to needle me, I hoped she would eventually get bored and leave. I had no intention of taking her out to dinner. I wanted to spend the evening alone.

About half an hour later she came bursting into my bedroom.

'You've got to come and see the news!' she said.

'Why?' I asked her irritably.

'The police are searching the woods near your wife's village.'

I got up and went next door and stared at the television screen. I still remember the image of those police. They moved slowly but there was something relentlessly methodical in the way they advanced. They thrashed the undergrowth with sticks and poked suspicious-looking piles of leaves or mould. They were accompanied by Alsatians on leashes. Wolf-like, these dogs sniffed and yelped and burrowed as they strained to get free. They seemed frenzied by the excitement of the chase. As they curled their lips and snarled their long wet tongues hung out of their mouths, raspberry-coloured against the whiteness of their spiky fangs.

The woods of Beckham looked bleak and murky. Sitting with Gloria in London and watching them being scoured by the police on the television, I would never have known I was looking at the same tract of trees that one could see from the window of Cressida's guest room. Scrub-infested and desolate, there was nothing to distinguish them from any other dank and overgrown woods.

'How do those police dogs know what they are tracking?' Gloria asked me.

'I imagine the police let them smell some of the child's clothing.'

'That's too ghastly,' Gloria said. 'That really makes me feel quite sick!'

I agreed with her. I too felt sickened by the sight of these men and dogs as they remorselessly covered every square yard of the gloomy wooded area. The faces of the police looked grim and tense. This was a mission they clearly disliked.

They also gave the impression they would not stop until they had found what they were looking for. They would walk those woods all day and if it was necessary they would walk them all night. If no trace of the child was uncovered, they'd enlarge their search and comb a wider area. They'd bring in low-flying helicopters in order to make aerial photographs of every field and lane, they'd examine all the local ditches, dredge every pond and lake.

'Oh, I hope to God they don't find her,' Gloria said. 'No, I don't mean that. I mean if they suddenly came across her, I hope they don't show us the poor little thing on the television. I don't think I could bear it.'

'That would be gruesome.' As I spoke I realised it was the first time I'd admitted that I thought it was extremely unlikely that Maureen Sutton was still alive.

Gloria and I drank some whisky but we were awkward and constrained. Gloria seemed to have forgiven me for having been insufficiently enthusiastic about her interview with the American actress, but the impact of what we had just seen on the television affected us so differently that we felt uncomfortable together for other reasons. Gloria wanted to talk about it and I only wanted to be left alone. I wanted to go back to my bedroom and read. If the little girl was dead, as now seemed likely, it was a tragedy but I couldn't see that there was much to say about it.

'Do you think they will ever find her?' Gloria asked me.

'I've no idea. How can I possibly tell?'

'The person who did it could have buried her. They could have buried her anywhere.'

'You've been reading too many detective stories.' I went over to Gloria and kissed her. I tried to feel her breasts, but she jerked away from me with a shiver of revulsion. I'd done something clumsy and inappropriate. Gloria rightly had sensed that I felt no desire for her at that moment but only a need to distract her. Her resentment and disgust made me feel crass and ashamed.

'You certainly are strange,' Gloria said. 'You don't seem to care what's happened to that child. I don't understand how you can be so indifferent. After all, you were down there in that village the night it happened.'

I wanted to deny that I was indifferent but I found it hard to do so. Gloria was becoming almost as obsessed by the disappearance of this child as my wife. Yet Gloria was childless and it was unlikely that she would ever have heard of the village of Beckham if my wife had not happened to live there. And still the case obviously haunted her. I'd never known her to become so emotionally involved with a news item. I couldn't understand the avid interest this case aroused in her and it made me impatient.

'It must have been a ghastly moment for the Suttons when the police asked them to produce some of their child's clothing,' Gloria said. 'It must have made them realise that there is not much hope they will ever see the poor little creature again.' I didn't answer. Why did she have to glory in every distasteful detail? It seemed presumptuous. I didn't feel that Gloria sitting drinking whisky in my flat in London had the right to reconstruct the painful experience of this unfortunate couple in Beckham.

'Perhaps we ought to go to bed,' I said. 'I want to get to work early in the morning.' Gloria shrugged her shoulders.

'I think I'll go back to my flat in that case.'

'Is there anything the matter?' I asked her.

'I'm upset. I find this case of the little girl upsetting. I'm sure your wife would understand exactly how I feel about it. I'm certain her reaction must be the same.'

Gloria had no idea how correct her guess was.

'If you are upset why don't you spend the night here with me?' I suggested.

Again she shrugged irritably as if she found it difficult to express what was troubling her.

'I don't feel like sex tonight,' she finally told me. 'This whole case is enough to put one off sex. If you think of that poor little child lying somewhere in the woods . . . It makes sex seem rather horrible.'

'We don't have to make love if you stay here tonight,' I protested. 'You make it sound as if I force you to do it against your will. If you were being fair you would admit that you can often be quite demanding . . .'

Gloria refused to smile. 'Tonight I want to be alone.' There was something extremely belligerent in the way she said this. She went and got her coat. She liked to wear long scarves. She found a long silk one and wrapped it three times round her neck. Every gesture she made was un-flurried and resolute.

Once Gloria had gone, I felt uncertain that I would ever see her again. I had always before believed that I controlled our relationship, that it was bound to continue for as long as I wanted it to. It was a shock to realise that it could be terminated at a moment's notice without my consent or approval.

I had seen cold revulsion in Gloria's eyes as she wrapped her scarf three times round her neck, as though trying to protect it. I couldn't understand what I'd done to deserve this loathing. Admittedly I had not been parti-cularly encouraging about her interview with the Amer-ican actress but I couldn't believe this was why she had been so anxious to leave my flat that evening. In the past I'd often shown very little interest in similar articles writ-ten by Gloria. This had always annoyed her. But our relationship still survived it. Now I was convinced it was over. When we had watched the television together and seen the police and their dogs scouring the Beckham woods, something disastrous had taken place between

Gloria and myself.

Superficially the evening had been quiet and uneventful. When we quarrelled our clash had been short-lived and muted. When Gloria and I parted, for once we had done so with dignity. There had been no high invective and histrionics. We had not interlocked our horns like fighting stags as we made wild threats of suicide and murder. Yet I was convinced this parting would be permanent. Alone in my flat I suffered from an infantile feeling of abandonment.

After about an hour I telephoned her. I hoped to reassure myself that my conviction that she had left me for ever was paranoid. When she answered it was not encouraging. She complained that I'd woken her. This was not a good sign. I didn't like to think she could get to sleep so quickly without me. Gloria was not overtly hostile but she sounded extremely bored and offhand. I got the impression she would have much preferred not to have heard from me. She made me feel tiresome, as if I'd dialled a wrong number.

I longed to ask her to get up and come back to my flat but I didn't dare suggest it. If I told her how much I wanted to see her I was certain she would say something rejecting.

'I miss you,' I said. Gloria didn't answer. 'I'd better let you sleep.' From then on our conversation degenerated and became an incoherent mumble in which the emotional undercurrents were obscured by grunts and coughs and banal inappropriate words.

Once we had rung off I tried to persuade myself that Gloria had sounded friendly. I reconstructed various things she had said and interpreted them in a way that made it possible for me to feel optimistic that she wanted our affair to continue exactly as it had before. I was still troubled that at no point had she said anything to suggest she wanted to see me again. Maybe Gloria was not feeling well. In the morning when she felt better her antagonistic attitude might change.

I took two sleeping pills and drank a tumbler of neat whisky. I was exhausted and yet too over-stimulated to sleep. Thinking about my life that night I saw it as a desolate range of mountains in which each pinnacle of failure led on to an even higher peak. My mind only seemed capable of selecting horrible memories from the past so that I vividly recalled every moment of humiliation and frustration that I'd endured from early childhood up to the present. With the distortion that depression induces I had the impression my experience had been one of unbroken pain.

When I finally slept it was not more pleasant. I dreamt I was in a wood. I was trying to hide but there were no bushes or undergrowth. The trees were saplings and their trunks were too thin and they were planted too far from each other to give any cover. Advancing slowly through the woods was a great line of police. They all had Alsatians. The baying of the dogs was a terrifying sound to hear. I had a feeling of pure white panic. I knew I'd never escape from those dogs. Wherever I tried to hide, I knew that in the end they would track me down. My panic was so violent it woke me. I wondered why the image of the police searching the Beckham woods had affected me so much that my sleeping mind had transformed it into a dream of terror.

In the morning I found Gloria's letter. She had delivered it by hand.

Dear Rowan,

This is not an easy letter to write. I will therefore try to come to the point as quickly as I can. I do not want to see you any more. You have set up a life for yourself that suits you. You have your work. You have your marriage, for it is obvious you never intend to divorce Cressida. All this is fine. But I do not feel there's much room in your life for me. At some point I would like to collect the clothes I have left in your flat. I'd prefer to do this when you are out as I can't see much point in our meeting. I'm afraid this letter may seem brutal but it says what I feel.

Yours,

Gloria

I read this letter many times. It didn't explain why she never wanted to see me again. She had always resented me for not divorcing Cressida. But what had made this old resentment become suddenly acute? When I'd gone down to Beckham last weekend, had Gloria felt that our relationship was becoming increasingly futile? Was that why she had decided to end it? I couldn't quite believe this. I suspected she was using my marriage as a convenient excuse to leave me. I wondered if she had started some new love affair. By reminding me that I'd made no attempt to free myself from my wife, she made it difficult for me to accuse her of fickleness and treachery. I felt that if Gloria had found some other man that she liked, she was cowardly not to tell me. Her letter was insulting it was so vague and dishonest.

The idea that Gloria had probably found a new lover was extremely painful to me. I kept trying to think of ways by which I could persuade her to give him up and come back to me. If I told her that I planned to divorce Cressida, would that change her attitude towards me? I'd always been frightened of marrying Gloria. But now she had left me I wanted her back so much that my old trepidations vanished.

My hand was shaking as I dialled Gloria's number. I was terrified a man's voice might answer her telephone. No one answered. Gloria apparently was out.

I was in a feverish state all morning. I telephoned Gloria repeatedly, but never reached her. I tried to work but found it impossible to concentrate. I was sitting in my study thinking about Gloria and trying to find an explanation for her behaviour when my telephone rang.

I was childishly excited as I rushed to answer it. I was

convinced it was Gloria ringing to tell me she didn't mean what she'd said in her letter.

'Rowan.' It was a woman's voice. But it wasn't Gloria's.

'Who is it?' I asked aggressively. My disappointment was acute.

'It's me. Surely you recognise my voice. It's Cressida.'

'Cressida!' I was astounded that it was her. Never once since we married had she rung me at my flat. It amazed me that she even knew my number.

'Cressida,' I said. 'How are you?'

'I'm desperately upset.'

'I'm so sorry. What's the matter?'

'The police have found the child's gym shoe.' Cressida sounded as if she was crying.

'Good Lord! Where did they find it?'

'In the woods. It's really horrible . . . Her gym shoe was covered with blood!'

I couldn't think of anything to say. My first reaction was to wonder what effect this news would have on Gloria. I feared it would increase our estrangement. Gloria was already critical of my inability to feel personally involved in this case. Now doubtless she'd find my response to this new and ugly piece of evidence was insufficiently emotional.

'Rowan,' Cressida said. 'Can I ask you something? I try not to ask you for much. But I'm doing it now because I'm desperate. Will you come down to Beckham tonight? I'm frightened to be alone.'

I told her my agent was arriving from the United States. I had to see him. My lie didn't sound in the least convincing. But I was determined not to go down to Beckham. I was already in a depressed state since Gloria's desertion and I feared that if I had to spend the evening with the forlorn little Mary Rose and the ghostly presence of little Maureen Sutton it might make me feel suicidal.

'I see,' Cressida said when she heard my excuse.

'If you lock the doors I don't think there's much you

need to be frightened of. I'll be coming down to see you at the weekend.'

'The weekend is very far away.'

I was ruthless. I gave my wife several reasons why it was so important that I saw my agent. While I was talking I kept thinking of the child's shoe. It was a vivid and repulsive image. It didn't make me want to cry like Cressida but I found I couldn't get it out of my mind.

This increased my horror of going down to Beckham. I didn't want to go near that deceptively peaceful little village which I now saw as an ugly and evil place.

'The beast that did it is still loose,' Cressida said.

'You mustn't think about that. The whole place must be swarming with police. You are quite well protected.'

'I don't feel protected,' Cressida said. 'I'm terrified. I'm terrified for Mary Rose.'

All the rest of the day I tried to speak to Gloria on the telephone but I had no success. Just before dinner I tried again and felt alarmed rather than pleased when she answered.

'I got your letter,' I muttered.

'It said everything that needs to be said. I don't know why you have rung me.'

'It didn't say everything,' I protested. 'In fact I found it cruel that you felt no need to explain why you want us to break up. Have I done something to make you angry with me? If so you ought to tell me.'

'You haven't done anything.'

'Why don't you want to see me then?'

'It's difficult to explain. I have personal reasons.'

'Don't you think we ought to meet? It's difficult to discuss these things on the telephone.'

'I don't want to meet. Didn't I make that clear in my letter?'

I went on pleading with Gloria. I became aggressive. I became self-pitying. Gloria stubbornly refused to see me. Finally I slammed down the receiver. I immediately regretted having done this. I knew she was not going to ring me back.

Later that evening I rang up Gloria's best friend and asked if I could come round to talk to her. Gloria and Valerie Middleton lunched together several times a week. They also had long gossipy conversations on the telephone every morning and exchanged confidences of an intensely intimate nature. Gloria and Valerie's relationship had always made me uneasy. I had never liked Valerie. I found her shallow and pointless. I was irritated by her gushing manner. She designed ugly modernistic jewellery. She was snobbish and constantly reminded one that she came from a very good family. Valerie was a plain young woman but she wore elaborate puffed-up hairstyles and heavy stage make-up and took such trouble with her appearance that sometimes she created the illusion that she was pretty. She admired Gloria and I always felt she envied her. As I had no respect for Valerie, I resented the way that my character and behaviour were presented to her for clinical analysis every morning.

I assumed that Valerie would know why Gloria had ended our relationship with such abruptness and I hoped she would explain.

When I arrived at her flat, Valerie was wearing silver pyjamas which were made of some kind of synthetic material. As usual she was heavily made up, and when she moved her eyes her false nylon eyelashes fluttered on her lids like the legs of an overturned beetle.

When I asked her why Gloria refused to see me, she looked shifty and embarrassed.

'You put me in a difficult position,' she said.

If Gloria had a new lover this would explain Valerie's embarrassment. When I asked her if this was true, she denied it. I couldn't tell if she was lying.

'Gloria is very worried about you,' Valerie said.

'And well she might be. The way she is treating me is really rather outrageous.'

'Gloria knows she has behaved badly. And she is quite

101

distressed about it. Gloria doesn't want to upset you. But there is nothing she can do about it.'

'If she's so distressed, she could have been a little nicer when I spoke to her on the telephone. And there is something she can do. She can tell me the real reason she has turned against me.'

'Gloria doesn't know how to explain.'

I felt enraged by Gloria's friend. The stupid girl was being maddeningly evasive. She seemed to enjoy tormenting me.

'Hasn't Gloria told you what's happened?' she asked.

'If she'd told me I wouldn't be here asking you to explain what's the matter with her!'

'If Gloria can't tell you herself, I really don't think that I can.'

Valerie's face looked malevolent with its mask of greasy make-up. Every word she said increased my suspicion that Gloria was in love with someone else. Valerie's small eyes stared at me through the spiky veil of her plastic eyelashes.

'You really mind losing Gloria, don't you?'

'Of course I mind.'

'That funny. I never felt she was all that important to you.'

'What made you think that?'

'She never seemed very happy when she was with you. I am going to be frank with you. As Gloria's friend I'm glad that she has left you.'

'Thank you for being so honest,' I said sarcastically.

'Gloria always felt that you were much more involved with your wife than you were with her.'

'Gloria was quite wrong. In fact I'm going to divorce my wife. If Gloria knew that, do you think her attitude towards me would change?'

'I doubt it,' Valerie said. 'From what Gloria's told me I think it's too late.'

'Please, Valerie. Please tell me what Gloria said to you about me.' It was demeaning to plead with this unsympathetic girl. However, it worked. She looked hesitant and then went and poured herself a drink.

'I shouldn't be the one to tell you. Gloria ought to do it herself.'

'I know that. But Gloria refuses to. You say that she doesn't know how to.'

'You aren't going to like what I'm going to tell you.'

'I know that. But I still want to know.'

'Gloria's turned off you.'

'How do you mean, turned off me?'

Valerie took a gulp of whisky. She looked flustered. 'Gloria has turned off you physically. She doesn't quite know why. She turns off people very suddenly. It's happened to her before. It's something she can't control. All she knows is that she never wants to go to bed with you again. The idea of sleeping with you makes her feel violently sick. She said it would be as disgusting as sleeping with her dribbling old smelly grandfather.'

I said nothing. I must have looked so stunned and unhappy that it made Valerie feel sorry for me. She went and got me a drink.

'I warned you that you weren't going to like being told this,' she said. 'You forced me to tell you.'

'Do you think Gloria will ever get over this sexual revulsion?'

'I wouldn't imagine so. Apparently at this point she feels that she couldn't bear to shake hands with you. That's quite extreme. Sex is a funny thing.'

'Gloria ought to have told me this,' I said bitterly.

'How could she tell you? It's such an insulting thing to tell anyone. Can't you understand? She knew it would hurt you.'

'Of course it hurts me. It's not very flattering to become the object of physical loathing. But I still want to go on seeing her. I'm not a brute. I'm quite prepared to respect Gloria's feelings. If she doesn't want to sleep with me I'll accept it. I'd still like to keep her friendship.'

Valerie shook her head. 'Gloria doesn't feel that would

103

be fair to you. A platonic relationship can only work if both parties want it to be that. Otherwise there is tension . . .'

'I'd better go,' I said. I couldn't bear to hear any more of Valerie's generalities.

'Where are you going?' she asked.

'Back to my flat.'

'Alone?'

'Obviously.'

Valerie leant back and with a languorous gesture she smoothed her hair which was like a yellow helmet stiff with peroxide and spray. As she lifted her arm, she made me aware of her large breasts rippling under her silver suit of peculiar glistening material, which was designed to look as if it was wet.

'You can stay here,' she said.

She gave me a suggestive look and flicked her eyelashes. I felt her flirtatiousness was aggressive. She wanted to make it clear that she did not feel she was being disloyal to her friend when she tried to seduce me. Since Gloria had discarded me, she saw me as fair game.

I told her that I preferred to go back to my own flat and pretended I hadn't notice how coquettish she was being. She didn't seem in the least offended. I felt her invitation had been some kind of trap, but she interested me so little I couldn't be bothered to work out why she had laid it.

Before I left, I asked her once again if Gloria had complained about anything I'd done or said in the last few days. I still wanted to believe there was some specific part of my behaviour that Gloria was objecting to.

'Gloria said she didn't like the way you treated your little girl,' Valerie said.

'How do you mean?' I asked sharply. 'What am I meant to have done to my little girl?'

Valerie made a vague shrugging gesture and said she didn't really know. All she'd gathered was that Gloria felt I ought to be more worried about my child, that she found it frightening I didn't seem at all concerned that she might be in danger living in a village where another small girl had just vanished in very suspicious circumstances.

'This is ridiculous,' I protested angrily. 'Gloria loves to exaggerate. My daughter's being looked after by my wife. She couldn't be in better care.'

Valerie gave me a patronising smile. 'Don't tell all this to me. Tell it to Gloria. I'm not worried about your daughter.'

'Gloria has no right to worry about my daughter either. My wife never lets her out of her sight.'

'That's not the point,' Valerie said. 'I've no idea what sort of house your wife lives in. But let me ask you this, is it a house someone could break into quite easily if they wanted to?'

My first instinct was to lie and say that Cressida's cottage was like a fortress. But I realised that it would not be very difficult to get into the living room from the garden. Someone would only have to smash the ground floor windows.

'I suppose most houses can be broken into if the person wishing to enter them is determined enough,' I admitted.

'That's just what I'm getting at.' Valerie looked triumphant.

'My wife has lived in Beckham for years and she's never had any trouble.'

'What a funny character you are!' Valerie gave an affected and mirthless laugh. 'You put on blinkers so that you can only see what it suits you to see. Surely you have to admit that it looks as if something extremely ugly has happened to that other little Beckham girl. I suppose you know they found blood all over her shoe.'

'I know,' I muttered uneasily. I wished she hadn't mentioned that shoe.

'Has it occurred to you that there may be a wildly dangerous psychopath roaming around at large in your wife's peaceful Kentish village? Any man who attacks a child has to be a maniac. And if he's a maniac, he may strike again . . .'

105

'Oh really, Valerie,' I interrupted her impatiently, 'that sounds like a banner headline in some sensational tabloid newspaper.' The more that she enjoyed dramatising the situation, the more I wanted to minimise it.

'Newspaper headlines report things that happen,' she continued stubbornly. 'Unfortunately insane killers often do strike again.'

'I must go home. It's late.' I couldn't bear to go on with this conversation any longer.

'I'm afraid I understand why Gloria finds you rather inhuman as a character,' Valerie said. 'I don't know much about your relationship with your wife. I've always assumed she must be some kind of mother figure to you, someone you can run home to from time to time when your other relationships get too hot for you to handle. But as I say, I'm only guessing about that . . . What I do find shocking is your attitude to your little daughter. I'm certain that most normal fathers would get into a frenzy if they knew there was a child killer operating within a thousand miles of where their daughter was living. Now when there is every likelihood that your poor wife's got a raving sex killer lurking in the local woods just waiting for his next victim, you don't seem to be the least bit troubled by it. I have to say I find that kind of indifference repellent. Apparently you quite often went down to stay with your family in the past when there was no particular reason except you knew it upset Gloria . But at a moment like this when your wretched wife might like the feeling that she has a man in the house, you prefer to stay swanning around in London.'

I made no protest as I listened to Valerie's censorious speech. There didn't seem to be much point in telling her that she'd got everything wrong – or almost everything. When she denounced me in this presumptuous fashion, she raised only one issue that troubled me. Could Cressida and my daughter really be in any danger? Both Valerie and Gloria seemed convinced that they were. But surely this was only a hysterical female fantasy.

Yet their insistence made me wonder if I could be deceiving myself. If I'd been a normal father and been deeply attached to the whey-faced Mary Rose, would I have been much more concerned for her safety and felt she was threatened, living in a village where there seemed to be a lot of evidence that an odious crime had been committed? If that little girl had been more precious to me would I have brought her up to London or gone down to Kent myself so that she'd have greater protection than was offered her by her fragile mother?

Valerie interrupted my thoughts. She asked me if I'd arranged for Cressida to have a patrol check.

'Patrol check?'

Valerie gave me an exasperated look. Her plucked eyebrows rose as she realised I had no idea what she was talking about.

'Surely you've informed the Beckham police that your wife is living all alone with a small child? I can't believe you haven't asked for a police patrol car to check on her several times a night?'

'I didn't know that one could ask the police to do that,' I murmured sheepishly.

'Of course you can ask them, under the circumstances.'

'I'm going down to stay in Beckham tomorrow,' I said quickly.

Valerie said she was glad to hear it. I found it curious that Gloria and Valerie had invented a Cressida who was an archetypal martyred wife so they could become her champions. It was as if they got some kind of thrill from identifying with this imaginary creature's plight.

When I got up to leave, Valerie accompanied me to the door, sidling up amorously in her slinky silver outfit. As I disappeared into the street, she blew me a kiss and called out 'Good luck'. Later I wondered what exactly she meant by that.

Chapter Eight

The telephone was ringing when I got back to my flat. It seemed to have a particularly menacing rasp as if it was trying to give a warning.

It was Cressida.

'Did you see the evening papers?'

'No.'

'They've found her.'

'Where?'

'In the woods. She'd been stabbed to death. Her body was hideously mutilated. Needless to say, she'd been sexually assaulted.'

I felt no surprise. It was as if I'd always known what Cressida was telling me. I had the unsettling sensation that I'd already seen the ghastly stab wounds on the child's small white body. I knew I ought to express some kind of horror but found it difficult to do so. It was as if this repulsive crime that had been committed in the Beckham woods had appalled me for so long it was now too late to give my disgust expression.

'The swine that did it had buried the poor little thing in some bushes,' Cressida said.

But why should this information also seem stale to me? Cressida, Mrs Butterhorn and Gloria had always assumed something unspeakable had happened to that little girl from the Beckham council estate. When they kept dropping their dark hints, had I unconsciously formed the ugliest possible picture of the child's death which now turned out to have been prophetic? Was this why the revolting details of her murder seemed familiar?

'God Almighty!' I said to Cressida.

'Can you imagine what that child must have gone through before she died?' she asked me. 'Can you imagine the terror she must have felt finding herself alone with that fiend in the woods?'

'I prefer not to think about it.'

'I've told Mary Rose,' Cressida said.

'You haven't!'

I was shocked. I couldn't believe it was right for her to have done this. It horrified me that Cressida, who was generally so protective of my daughter, should have told her about the killing of the child. Surely this would have an extremely disturbing effect on someone of Mary Rose's age.

'I had to tell her,' Cressida said.

'Why did you have to? I'm sure we could have easily concealed the whole thing from her.'

'I didn't want to conceal it from her. I wanted her to know exactly what happened to Maureen Sutton so that she would be warned.'

I gave up. It was useless to protest.

'You must be shaken by this whole awful business,' I said. 'I'll come down and see you tomorrow.'

'Couldn't you come tonight?'

'Cressida! Are you mad? Do you realise it's two o'clock in the morning?'

My wife had ceased to be at all considerate and this I found disturbing.

'I've hardly slept since that child disappeared. The only time I get a wink of sleep is if Mary Rose keeps guard.'

'How do you mean?' I asked.

'Mary Rose sits up for a couple of hours every night. That's when I take a short nap. I've explained to her that if she hears a footstep or anyone moving about in the garden, she is to wake me immediately.'

'Is it good for such a young child to be up at night?'

'It's not good for her at all. But other things could happen to her which would be much more harmful.'

Again I couldn't argue. But I still found the idea of my daughter sitting up alone at night in the cottage disquieting. It appalled me that Cressida who was such a devoted mother would make her do this. Surely it wasn't healthy for a child to be put on guard so that she listened to every rustle in the garden with petrified apprehension.

'At the beginning I stayed up all night myself,' Cressida continued as if to excuse her behaviour, 'but I found I couldn't keep it up. I was too exhausted in the daytime to be able to give Mary Rose the necessary care. That's why I now ask her to take over. If I can just get two hours of uninterrupted sleep, I find I can function perfectly well.'

It made sense but only within the framework of Cressida's eccentric logic.

'Would you like me to arrange for the police to do a security check on the cottage?' I asked her. 'Apparently we could ask them to send a patrol car to check that you are all right. We could ask them to come round several times a night.'

She said that would not be much use. Once the patrol car had gone away, she would feel she still had to keep herself awake. Only if the police were to stay in her cottage all night long could she relax. I told her that I didn't think we could ask them to do that. After all, it was not a real emergency. There was no reason to believe that my wife and Mary Rose were in any particular danger.

Cressida said she doubted that little Maureen Sutton had felt she was in special danger when she had gone out last Saturday evening to play. I agreed, but begged her not to get too over-excited by the situation. She seemed convinced the Beckham child-killer had singled out Mary Rose to be his next victim. I reminded my wife that the police were launching a nationwide search for this man. If he had any sense, he would go into hiding in the near future. I felt it was most unlikely he would try to repeat his crime.

110

Cressida said she couldn't understand why I was so confident that the killer's future actions would be rational. Did I realise the savagery with which the child had been attacked? The police were convinced they were searching for a vicious lunatic. If the horrible creature was insane, who could predict what his next move would be? I couldn't argue. All I could do was to remind her that I would be seeing her tomorrow. After that I said good-night.

In the morning the crime was reported in the news-papers. I saw the headline 'The Beast of Beckham makes brutal attack on child'. The black print of these words seemed to turn scarlet as I stared at them and I had the odious feeling that they were written in blood. I couldn't bear to read the account. I threw the newspaper into a rubbish bin.

Before I left for the country, I telephoned Gloria. I tried to be controlled and casual. If I became emotional and bombarded her with recriminations and entreaties, she would find my pressure burdensome and I feared this would only strengthen her resolve never to see me again. I therefore made no suggestion that we meet in the near future. I told her I was going down to Beckham to stay with my wife as I felt someone should be with her at this moment because she was terrified at night and had been unable to sleep ever since the brutal slaying of the child.

Gloria said she was not surprised that Cressida was frightened. She herself would be scared out of her wits if she were living in a village where something so abomi-nable had just happened. She had read the details of the killing in the newspapers and they had made her blood run cold. If the man who had done it was caught, she would like to gouge his eyes out − hanging would be much too good for him.

Gloria reminded me that I'd been staying in Beckham the night the child had been assaulted. What had I done that evening? Had I seen anyone suspicious prowling around? If I had noticed anything that might have some

111

bearing on this ghastly case, she felt it was my duty to inform the police.

I didn't want to tell Gloria that the night the child had been attacked I'd been so revoltingly drunk that I remembered nothing about the whole evening. As Gloria was already hostile towards me, I felt it would be unwise to admit that my behaviour on that occasion had been uniquely discreditable. I therefore told her I'd noticed nothing that could be remotely connected with the case. I lied and said that I'd stayed at home in the cottage and watched television with Mary Rose.

Gloria was so affected by little Maureen Sutton's murder that when we discussed this topic she spoke to me naturally, glad to find anyone who was prepared to discuss it. Once we left the subject, our conversation immediately became awkward and constrained and beneath our polite exchange there was the tension of many complicated feelings which were not being expressed.

Gloria asked me how my work was going. I knew she wasn't interested. She only asked the question to prevent an uneasy silence. I said it was going well, although this was the reverse of the truth. Ever since I'd received Gloria's dismissive letter, I'd felt increasingly discouraged about my current project. The realisation that I no longer felt I understood Gloria at all had made me lose all confidence that I could write anything very valuable about Hertha Ayrton. When I re-read my notes, I got the disheartening impression that I had merely listed the achievements of this pioneer scientist, but the woman herself was missing because I understood nothing of the dynamics of her character which had made her feats possible.

I didn't tell Gloria this in case it made her feel that I was trying to blame her for my collapse of confidence. In studiedly offhand tones I asked her what she was doing this weekend. She told me she was going to stay with some friends in Wales. This jarred for I found it painful to realise that from now on her plans and movements no longer would have any connection with mine. I would have liked to have told her how much I wished I was going with her instead of going down to stay in Beckham with my jumpy wife. But I just wished her a pleasant weekend and said I would speak to her on Monday and give her a report on any developments in the Kentish murder case. I longed to have an excuse to keep in contact with Gloria and I hoped her curiosity about the case would make her agree to speak to me.

It was ironic that the death of this unknown child had become the only issue on which we could communicate with any ease. And I had the suspicion that it was this same death that was in some subtle way responsible for the aversion Gloria had developed towards me. It was almost as if Gloria by some irrational quirk had started to associate me with the bloody killing that had taken place in the Beckham woods.

Chapter Nine

I arrived at Cressida's cottage in the evening. It was almost as dirty and disorderly as the house of Mrs Butterhorn. There were used dishes piled up in the kitchen sink. The floor had not been mopped. Nothing seemed to have been dusted or tidied and I missed the usual smell of furniture polish. The whole place was cold and desolate because none of the fires had been lit.

When I rang it took a long time for Cressida to answer. She had installed a peephole system on the front door and she was peering through it to see who was there. She had also put on two new extra heavy bolts and it seemed to take ages before she opened them. When she finally opened up, I noticed iron grilles had been fitted across all the ground floor windows.

'I've changed the lock,' she said.

'You'd better give me a new key.'

'I didn't have any extra ones cut.'

She had lost a lot of weight and she had the emaciated semi-transparent look of someone recovering from a long debilitating illness.

'We had another ghastly night,' she said.

'I'm sorry. Did anything special happen?'

'Nothing happened exactly. But there was the most fearful wind and all night long I kept hearing that child screaming for help in the woods. The wind seemed to blow her screams towards the cottage. You can't imagine what it was like. It was one of the most blood-curdling sounds I've listened to in my whole life. Mary Rose heard it too.

She was shaking so badly I had to take the poor little thing into my bed. I sat up with her and kept my arm round her until morning . . .'

'Cressida . . .' I said. 'This is all in your imagination. I understand that this appalling case has had a very disturbing effect on you. But for the sake of Mary Rose you ought to make some attempt to pull yourself together.'

Cressida was in a much worse state than I had feared. I was polite to her because politeness was my armour but my cool display of good sense concealed a rage so intense I experienced it as a physical symptom. It seemed exactly like red-hot coal that had become lodged in my windpipe. It burned and it burned. All I craved was ice-cold water. Never before had my wife with her lily-coloured skin and pale unfocused eyes seemed quite so repugnant to me. I detested her for forcing me to listen to this disgusting and macabre fantasy. It was curious because the wave of murderous anger that overcame me was not fury on my own behalf. For the first time in my life I felt violently angry on behalf of Mary Rose. I hadn't seen the child since I had arrived in the cottage. I assumed she was crouching somewhere upstairs, quivering and mute. I dreaded seeing her. But the anger I felt on her behalf was still genuine. How could Cressida, who claimed to be brimming over with maternal love, justify what she had done to Mary Rose last night? Surely there could be nothing more terrifying for a sensitive little girl than to be kept up all night by a mother who maintained that every gust of wind carried the shriek of the slaughtered child from the council estate. My wife's behaviour was self-indulgent and cruel to the point of being criminal.

'Is there any whisky in the house?' I asked her.

'I'm afraid I forgot to get any. I've had more important things to think about.'

'In that case I think I'll drive over to the Red Lion and pick up a bottle.' I wanted to get out of the cottage and rid myself of my anger which was still burning like a live coal in my windpipe.

115

'Will you come back immediately?' Cressida asked me as I was leaving. 'Promise me you won't stay out late drinking. Mary Rose and I really need to get some sleep.'

I promised her that I wouldn't stay out late. She had never made this kind of demand on me before. She sounded frantic, as if she felt it was a matter of life and death that I return very soon. To my horror I saw there were tears in her eyes. After I'd gone out, I heard the clang and rattle of her closing all the new heavy bolts.

As I got into my car, I had a longing to drive back to London. There was no need to say goodbye to Cressida. There was nothing she could do if I decided to vanish. The idea of spending the night in the cottage was insufferable. All the new grilles and bolts by which she had secured it gave me the sense that I would be imprisoned if I stayed there, trapped with all the hallucinatory terrors which were teeming in Cressida's disordered mind.

Just when I'd decided to make my escape, I thought of Mary Rose. I remembered the way she had stood at her bedroom window in the past and greeted me as my car scrunched on to the gravel patio, waving with her limp little hand.

I remembered the first time that I saw her when I visited Cressida in the hospital a few days after she had given birth. Mary Rose was lying in a cot beside her mother's bed. Her face was purple and she was screaming her head off. Her stomach was knotted with anguish and stuck out in such a hard ball that the little creature looked as if she was pregnant. Her puny little legs and arms were waving frenziedly in the air.

'Is she all right?' I asked Cressida. The infant looked to me as if it was having a fit.

'She's being naughty,' her mother said with a smile. Cressida was in a strangely serene and exalted mood as if she was looking down to earth from some lofty position on a cloud.

'She wants to be fed. But she's got to wait,' Cressida said.

'Couldn't you feed her?' I asked. I found the screams intolerable. They drilled my nerves. I could hardly bear to stay in the room.

'Of course she can't be fed. She's got to learn to get on to a proper feeding schedule.'

I left soon after that, pretending that I had an appointment. I'd experienced none of the reactions that I believed to be appropriate to a father seeing his first child. I felt no wonder or pride when I was shown this ugly little raw-looking and howling baby. My only desire was to get myself out of earshot of her screams.

'Isn't she a lovely little thing?' one of the nurses said to me.

Later, when I was driving back to my flat, I found myself looking at the faces of the people in the street. I deliberately picked out all the casualties, the crazy, drunken ones who cursed or muttered, the unfortunates who could hardly walk, they appeared to have been so defeated by disease and poverty and pain. At some point far back in the past someone must have admired all these unlucky-looking people. Someone must have said they were lovely babies. These thoughts hardly helped me feel particularly elated by the birth of Mary Rose.

Yet when I was driving to get a bottle of whisky from the Red Lion, I suddenly felt convinced that it would be immoral for me to return to London and leave my daughter alone at night in the cottage with her mother. Cressida seemed to have become totally unbalanced since the murder of Maureen Sutton and it was impossible to predict what she might say or do. Her determination to make Mary Rose aware of all the more horrendous aspects of this gruesome killing was proof that in her present state of hysteria she had temporarily ceased to care how much she terrified and upset the child. I resolved to stay overnight in the cottage although the prospect was extremely unappealing. I hoped my presence would enable Cressida to get a good night's sleep and help her to regain her composure. I was prepared to stay only one night in the cottage to try to help her get back her mental equilibrium. But if my wife didn't seem to be more in control by the morning so that she no longer made me feel it was irresponsible and heartless to leave Mary Rose alone in her care, I didn't know what was going to happen.

Chapter Ten

Beckham was ominously hushed that evening as I drove towards the pub. The whole village had a sinister and throbbing atmosphere. It was as if its inhabitants were frightened to leave their houses.

Police cars kept circling round the green. I deliberately drove at a snail's pace as they kept swooshing past me flashing their blue rotating lights. The silence was occasionally broken by the noise of walky-talkies. The presence of so many police should have been reassuring but it made me apprehensive. I thought at any moment they might stop me. It made me feel I was breaking some kind of curfew.

The Red Lion was not nearly as full and noisy as usual. There were a few men drinking by the bar. They were subdued. No one was laughing or making jokes. As I came through the door, they all stopped talking and stared at me. I disliked the fear and hostility with which I was examined. I'd always been a misfit in this pub community. My appearances at the Red Lion were irregular whereas most of the other customers were to be seen there almost every night. No one was quite sure where I came from or what I was doing there. If I'd tried to ingratiate myself with the other drinkers by buying them rounds of drinks, I might have become less unpopular. But I'd never been friendly or generous. I'd drunk too much alone in a desperate rather than a convivial way and now that there was an unsolved crime in the village, I could tell by the grim looks that greeted me as I entered that I was a figure who was regarded with suspicion and dread.

I went over to the bar and ordered a whisky.

'Have you heard what's happened here?' the landlord asked me. I told him that I'd heard.

'For the last few nights this place has been almost empty. An atrocious thing like this is very bad for business. No one feels like going out to enjoy themselves. Everyone has it on their mind. It casts a shadow . . .'

It appeared that yesterday he'd been called down to the police station for questioning. 'It wasn't a personal kind of questioning if you understand, Sir. I'm lucky in that way. No one needs to ask me where I was at the exact time that the killing took place. I was right here behind my bar where everyone could see me!'

'What did the police want to know?' I asked him.

'They asked me all sorts of general questions about my customers. They wanted to be told who came in that evening - what time they left. All that sort of thing. They were interested to hear if any strangers came in for a drink, any seedy types who struck me as peculiar.'

'What did you tell them?'

'I told them that I have a very decent and well-to-do clientele here in the Red Lion. Most of my customers are solid people I've known all my life.'

The landlord of the Red Lion twirled his gingery moustache with a self-congratulatory gesture.

'We rarely have seedy types in here. That's what I told them. If they are looking for suspicious characters, I suggested they ask a few questions in the pubs near the council estate . . .'

I left him and went and sat down in a booth. I'd promised Cressida I'd return immediately but I wanted to stay for a few minutes in the pub although I felt far from comfortable there and only the landlord seemed well-disposed towards me because I'd spent a lot of money buying drinks through the years.

'Long time, no see!' Someone had come up behind me and was slapping me on the back. I turned round expecting to see a man and realised that this booming greeting had come from Mrs Butterhorn.

'What a jump you gave,' she said complacently. 'Your nerves can't be very good. Did you think you were being arrested?'

Her appearance was just as absurd as usual. She was dressed in oilskins like the captain of a trawler, and her stout little legs were encased in long grey rubber waders. She sat down beside me and offered to buy me a drink. I refused because I didn't want to feel in the smallest degree indebted to her.

She went waddling off to the bar in her ludicrous waders. She returned with a large brandy and soda and sat down holding her legs wide apart.

Her toad-like eyes examined me. 'You are being very abstemious this evening.' I grunted vaguely. What did she expect me to say?

'The last time I saw you in this pub you weren't being so careful. Oh my God, you were pickled, if you don't mind me saying so! That must have been about a week ago. In fact it was last Saturday. Come to think of it, it was the same evening that the child disappeared . . .'

'I wish you wouldn't remind me. It's not an evening I'm proud of.'

'I don't wonder,' she said. 'I was sitting in a booth and I was watching you. I don't think I've ever seen a man drink quite so much in such a short time. You were standing over there by the bar and you were knocking back the whiskies one after another. You drank them down in one quick gulp like people drink medicine.'

'I don't want my behaviour described to me.'

Mrs Butterhorn leant over and gave me a clap on the shoulder.

'I've nothing against drinking.' Her smile was tolerant. 'I'm very fond of the bottle myself. I make no attempt to hide it. When I was married to Mervyn I just had the odd glass of wine and the pre-dinner sherry. Since Mervyn's death, I get sloshed when I want to get sloshed. And no

121

one's going to stop me!'

I'd always felt that just as she had a green finger touch in her garden, Mrs Butterhorn had much the same gift in her conversation. Whatever topic she chose to talk about immediately budded and threw out tiny febrile shoots of boredom. As she discoursed on her drinking habits, I felt that once again she had made something mildly uninteresting flower into something blazingly dull.

'As I say, I'm no puritan when it comes to the booze,' she continued. 'But to be frank, I didn't like to see you in the state you were in the other night. You seemed to be trying to smash yourself unconscious. When I take one too many, I do it in order to enjoy life a bit more. But you got yourself drunk in a ferocious kind of way. It made me wonder if things were happy in your home.'

I shrugged irritably. I was extremely sorry to hear that Mrs Butterhorn had been in the pub when I had made such a fool of myself. It was humiliating to have been observed by her, especially as I knew she would use any excuse to try to make me talk about my marriage. Never had I felt less like discussing it than I felt that evening.

'There's something I want to say to you.' Mrs Butterhorn leant towards me and lowered her booming voice so that it became a gruff whisper. 'I know you may find this impertinent. But I have to say it. I feel very worried about your wife . . .'

'What's wrong with my wife?' I became immediately defensive. 'Obviously Cressida has been very shaken up by this ghastly business with the local child. But I don't find that extraordinary.'

'No, there's nothing odd about that,' Mrs Butterhorn quickly agreed with me. 'It has shaken me up myself. It's hard to believe something so terrifying could have happened here. When I first moved to Beckham it seemed such an adorable little village. I used to think of it as one of the last strongholds of English civilisation. I get up early because I like to work in my garden . . . Sometimes in the past when I've looked over my fence and seen the

122

Beckham green spread out like an emerald glistening with morning dew and behind it the façades of those pretty little rose-coloured houses, I've felt I lived in one of the most delightful spots on earth. Nothing much has changed her since the eighteenth century.'

'The council estate doesn't look exactly eighteenth-century.' I always mentioned the council estate when anyone became too lyrical about Beckham.

Mrs Butterhorn gave an uneasy little twitch as if she'd been stung by a horse-fly. 'I'm the last person to defend the council estate. As far as I'm concerned, the people who gave planning permission and allowed that monstrosity to be erected were criminals. If I had my way, I'd have them all shot! That used to be lovely rolling farm-land until those ghastly buildings started going up. They destroyed beautiful meadowland in order to create a man-made breeding ground for squalor, disease and crime. And now that poor little girl has been hacked to death, we see the results . . .'

'There's no evidence that her killer comes from the council estate,' I protested.

'If he's a local man as the police seem to think, more than likely he comes from the council estate.'

'I must go home.' This opinionated woman made me feel exhausted.

Mrs Butterhorn said she understood I didn't want to leave my wife alone in the state she was in. Once again she said that she was worried about her.

She clearly longed to gossip about Cressida. I found this annoying and intrusive and would have liked to have snubbed her by refusing to pay any interest. But my curiosity was aroused and I asked her why she felt concerned.

Mrs Butterhorn said that although she had been Cressida's closest neighbour for nearly seven years, she had never really spoken to her until yesterday. Cressida had always been perfectly polite in the past and had greeted her pleasantly whenever they ran into each other, but Mrs

Butterhorn had never had the impression my wife was keen for the relationship to become any more intimate. Cressida had not been exactly stand-offish but if Mrs Butterhorn invited her for a drink or a meal, she invariably refused, using the pretext that Mary Rose was unwell.

'As I've always been a person who likes to keep herself to herself, I respect those who prefer to keep the rest of the world at a certain distance.' Mrs Butterhorn seemed to be blithely unaware that she sometimes startled me by her dishonesty. She claimed that it had not offended her that Cressida had never once asked her inside the cottage. She had accepted that my wife was not a gregarious young woman. She admired her for being an excellent mother who gave undivided attention to her child.

Yesterday Mrs Butterhorn had got a nasty shock. She had been doing some planting in her garden when Cressida came out into the back yard of our cottage. She then went to the fence and stood there looking over it at Mrs Butterhorn as if she wanted to say something to her. Mrs Butterhorn had greeted her casually and asked her how she was. She noticed that Cressida seemed to be very nervously excited and she had an odd expression in her eyes.

My wife suddenly asked her if she would like to come over and have a cup of tea. Mrs Butterhorn was amazed and accepted at once. After so many years as Cressida's closest neighbour, she couldn't imagine why she'd been offered this hospitality.

She went next door and Cressida had given her such a fright.

'What did she do?' I was impatient for Mrs Butterhorn to get to the point.

'I wasn't shocked by anything she did. But I have to admit I was quite horrified by something she told me she'd done.'

'And what was that?'

'She told me she had gone up to the woods . . .'

'The woods!'

'Yes. The woods where they found the dead child.'

'When did she do that? What on earth was she doing there?'

'She went the day after it happened. She wanted to look at the place where they found the body.'

'God Almighty!' I said. 'Why did she want to do that?'

Mrs Butterhorn drank her brandy. She apologised for telling me something so disturbing. She could see by my face that I was as shattered as she was. Ever since Cressida told her what she had done, she had been unable to get it out of her mind. She felt it was her duty to inform me. She was relieved to have met me in the pub, for she'd been frightened she would never get the proper opportunity.

'Your wife has always struck me as rather a solemn young woman,' she continued. 'But when she described what she'd done up in the woods, she kept smiling. She seemed to be extremely pleased with herself. It wasn't natural the way she smiled. I didn't like it. Tell me, does she often smile?'

'No,' I said. 'She rarely smiles.'

'The area where the killing took place had been cordoned off by the police. Apparently your wife had quite a lot of difficulty persuading them to let her through. She told them a whopping great lie – she was cunning and managed to catch them off their guard. It seems the police lost their heads and they allowed her to do what she wanted. She kept smiling when she told me this. She seemed to feel she had been very clever indeed!'

'How did my wife get past the police?' As I asked the question I realised I didn't really care to know.

'She said she was a close relative of the murdered child. She asked the police if she could say a quick prayer on the spot where the child met her end.'

'Jesus Christ! How could the police have been so idiotic as to go along with that? They really are a bunch of heavy-footed fools!' All the disapproval that I felt for Cressida's inexplicable behaviour turned into a feeling of

125

rage against the police.

Mrs Butterhorn said she didn't blame them. They had probably never had such an unusual request before. It obviously never occurred to them that Cressida's story was a lie. Apparently my wife had been crying her eyes out when she asked to be allowed to say a prayer for Maureen Sutton. Mary Rose had been sobbing too. Clearly the police had been affected by their grief and had not liked to turn them away. They may well have found my wife's request eccentric but they probably saw no harm in letting her do what she wanted. Presumably they had already taken footprints and combed the area for clues.

'So my wife took Mary Rose when she went to the woods? And you say that Mary Rose was sobbing?' It was inevitable that Cressida would have taken my daughter. Once again I experienced the burning sensation that I had felt earlier talking to Cressida in the cottage.

Cressida had described my daughter's reaction with approval. She had not seemed perturbed by the fact that Mary Rose had become hysterical when she was shown the exact place where the child had perished. On the contrary, it seemed to gratify her. The police had drawn a chalk mark where the rape had taken place. It was obvious there had been a horrible struggle. There was blood all over the ground, and it was indented as if at some point the killer had lain with his full weight on the wretched child. The police had told her there also had been a moment when he had gone berserk for her body had been slashed repeatedly with a sharp knife and specks of blood were to be found at a great distance from where the actual assault had occurred. After the child was dead, he had thrown her into the nearest rhododendron bush. He had made no particular attempt to hide the traces of his crime. The police believed they were looking for a man who was of a low-grade brutish intelligence.

'I'm sorry. I can't bear to talk about it any more . . .' Mrs Butterhorn slumped forward over the small steel table that held her brandy. She bowed her head with

126

its badly cut grey hair and hid her face in her stumpy-fingered hands.

I patted the shoulder of her oilskin jacket. She had always seemed such an indomitably robust character that it embarrassed me to see her cry.

'I'm sorry,' she repeated in muffled tones. 'I've not been myself in the last week.'

I offered to get her another brandy. She slowly raised her head and nodded, giving me a wan smile. Her thyroid eyes were watery and inflamed.

When I returned from the bar she apologised once again for having broken down. She rummaged for a handkerchief in the inner pockets of her seaman's jacket. I expected her to produce something huge and masculine and was taken aback when she fished out a little ladies' hanky embroidered with daisies.

'I've been going through a crisis recently.' She sniffed and dabbed her eyes. 'I've decided to sell my house.'

'You can't do that. You can't give up your garden!' I felt that for Mrs Butterhorn this would be a suicidal act.

'I don't care about my garden any more. I've done what I can to make it lovely. When my house is sold the next owners can enjoy my work. They'll probably neglect it and it will soon revert to a jungle infested with weeds. Why should I care? I won't be there to see . . .'

'Where are you going to move to?'

She gave a hopeless shrug. Her bulging eyes looked desperate. 'I don't know . . . I may go back to London.'

'I thought you hated living in London.'

'That's true. I detest living in London. But now I loathe living in Beckham almost more.'

'Is it to do with the murder of the Sutton child?'

She nodded miserably. 'The atmosphere is unspeakable here. You only arrived this evening. You probably haven't had the time to notice. It's the ghastly suspicion . . . I can feel it now in this pub. Every time a man comes through the door, you look at him and you wonder . . . Every woman keeps looking at every man.

127

Every man keeps looking at every other man. It's becoming like a nightmare. Human beings can't live with so much mistrust and uncertainty . . .'

'I've felt it,' I said. 'I can see why you don't like it. The mood in this village is certainly not at all pleasant.'

Ever since Mrs Butterhorn had cried, she had ceased to boom at me. Her bristling self-assertiveness had left her and I liked her much better than I ever had before.

'After Mervyn died,' she said, 'I enjoyed my independence. I never felt a moment's loneliness. I got on with the life I'd chosen for myself. Now all that has changed.'

'How do you mean?'

'I'm frightened,' she said. 'I'm scared to death when I'm alone in my house. I keep telling myself not to be foolish. A man who goes for a child of Maureen Sutton's age isn't likely to go for an old bag like me. But when night starts to fall, I don't see it like that. I get this awful feeling that something evil is prowling around outside in the dark . . .'

'Can't you get someone to stay with you?'

'Whom would I ask?' She looked increasingly forlorn. 'You know Tom Crake. He's the old fellow who helps me with the garden. He's a lazy old bastard. You have to keep after him to stop him slacking, but he knows a lot about plants. I've offered Tom Crake £50 a night if he'll sleep in my house.'

'Has he agreed?'

She shook her head. Tom Crake apparently lived with his sister, an elderly spinster who was very highly strung. Although she would have been glad to get the money, she refused to let her brother stay with Mrs Butterhorn. She said she would die of terror if he left her alone in their cottage at night.

Why didn't Mrs Butterhorn ask Tom Crake's sister to sleep in her house as well? In that way everyone would have company. As I made this sensible suggestion, I found myself nursing the crazy hope that Cressida and Mary Rose could also move in with her and I then would be able to return to London.

Mrs Butterhorn said she was too old to share her house with other people. Since Mervyn died, she had never tried to maintain a well-run establishment. She'd had no interest in keeping up with the Joneses. If she lived in a bit of a pigsty that was her business. What she had loved about her life in Beckham was the feeling she was totally self-reliant. However, in the last week she had realised that she was not the courageous and independent character she had always thought herself to be. This had been very painful.

If her fears at night were so great that she was willing to pay strangers to sleep under the same roof, she saw no point in remaining in Beckham. Tom Crake and his difficult old sister would get on her nerves in no time. They would make her feel her house was no longer her own.

'But your garden . . .' I protested. 'Somehow I feel that it's a crime for you to abandon your garden. Won't it break your heart to leave it?'

She shook her head. I was frightened that she was going to cry again. Yesterday when she tried to do some planting, she had started to hate her garden. It seemed much too near to the Beckham woods. She could see the tops of the trees over her fence. She was aware of them all the time.

'Yesterday I lost my faith in gardening like people lose their faith in God. I suppose I've always been rather a naive type of person. I once saw gardening as the supremely innocent occupation. You help beautiful things to grow. I thought there was nothing less harmful than that.'

'Why do you see gardening as harmful now?' I asked.

Her face twitched irritably. My stupidity annoyed her.

'I only see it as harmful in the sense that it can't prevent harm from being done. Yesterday I felt it was a totally futile activity. What's the point in spending a morning tying sacks over your azalea plants in order to protect them from the frost if you can't prevent a child from being lured to her death in the neighbouring woods?'

129

'You shouldn't think like that,' I said. It saddened me to hear Mrs Butterhorn was selling her house and moving back to London. Despite her manly attire, her butch grey hair and her weatherbeaten skin she suddenly seemed young and vulnerable. This woman whom I'd always seen as some kind of ancient warrior, for a moment became a terrified and troubled little girl.

'Let me ask you something,' I said to her. 'My wife as you know has a maniacal preoccupation with the Sutton case. Her hysteria on the subject becomes infectious. I wondered if there was anything she said that made you feel you wanted to get rid of your house and go back to London.'

Mrs Butterhorn frowned as she reflected. Finally she nodded. Her conversation with Cressida yesterday had been profoundly disturbing. She couldn't understand why Cressida had chosen her to be her confidante. It was the last thing she wanted.

'I felt like an impaled insect,' Mrs Butterhorn said. 'Your wife just transfixed me with those funny light blue eyes. She kept talking and talking and she was speaking much too fast. It was like listening to a record played at the wrong speed.'

Mrs Butterhorn once again got out her dainty handkerchief and wiped away a tear.

'Your wife seemed to be asking for my approval. That's what made me feel there was something hideously wrong with her. When she described all the blood she had seen in the woods, my stomach started curdling. She reconstructed the whole crime. I really thought I was going to be sick on the floor. She made the whole thing seem unbearably vivid . . .'

'I'm afraid my wife has never been very sensitive to the effects that her concerns have on others.'

'That's what I mean,' Mrs Butterhorn said. 'I don't think she realised she had shocked me at all. I've never been a mother . . . I don't know much about the upbringing of children. But to have taken your poor little girl up to the scene of the killing . . . To have pointed out every bloodstain . . . To have made her pray by the bushes where they discovered the body . . . In my opinion any mother who would do that to her child is some kind of fiend!'

'Did you see my daughter yesterday, Mrs Butterhorn? I wondered how she seemed to you.'

'I never saw her. The poor little mite was locked upstairs in her bedroom. I suppose you know that your wife has put a huge bolt on her door? She keeps her shut up all day. She says it's not safe to allow her to go roaming around. She has to know exactly where she is . . .'

'Mrs Butterhorn . . .' I said. 'I'm going to be frank with you. I find my wife's recent treatment of my daughter every bit as troubling as you do. I'm going to ask you a difficult question. Do you think at this moment my wife is entirely sane?'

When I asked her this I was hoping for reassurance. I was asking this woman whom I barely knew a question I'd never before dared to ask myself.

Mrs Butterhorn paused as if she needed time to reflect before she gave me a serious answer.

'I was certainly very glad to get away from her. Her whole demeanour struck me as distinctly unnatural. She kept moving about and waving her arms while she was talking. And then her eyes had this horrible snake-pit expression. To be honest with you, I wondered if your wife was taking drugs . . .'

I told Mrs Butterhorn I felt this was extremely unlikely. My wife was much too puritanical. She was the kind of person who refuses to eat refined sugar because it is bad for the human body. As I kept protesting that Cressida would never dream of taking drugs, I wondered why I dared to feel so certain of this. Did I really know what my wife was like? Did I have any idea what she was capable of doing?

'Shall I tell you why I put my house on the market yesterday afternoon?' Mrs Butterhorn said. 'It wasn't just

131

because I felt it was too near to the Beckham woods. You may think I'm mad. But I decided I had to sell my house immediately because it was too near to your wife's cottage.'

'I don't think you are insane,' I said. 'Why do you think I am sitting here in this pub? It's very pleasant to talk to you. But I'm only really lingering on here because I dread going back to spend the night in that cottage.'

Mrs Butterhorn looked aghast. Her protruding eyes examined me. Because they stuck out from her head, she appeared to have better vision than other people.

'You are not saying that you feel your wife might be dangerous . . .'

'How do you mean, dangerous? Of course I don't mean that. You speak of poor Cressida as if she was a dog with the rabies. My wife is a very frightened woman, Mrs Butterhorn. You can understand that. Apparently you share many of her fears. I have to admit it is a strain for me to be with her at this point. I feel inadequate. I find it difficult to say the right thing to reassure her. If only the police would pick up the killer . . . Then she'd calm down and be more like her old self . . .'

I wanted to minimise the impact of what I'd confessed to Mrs Butterhorn. She remained thoughtful, staring at me with her bulbous eyes.

'Why do you think your wife will become calmer once the police find the killer?' she asked me.

'Obviously that would make her feel much better. Once they pick him up she'll cease to live in a state of terror.'

'I think you may be being rather naive about that,' Mrs Butterhorn said.

Outside the pub a police car roared by with its siren screaming. She gave a shiver.

'I'm moving to London next week. I'm packing up a few things and I'm getting myself a room in an hotel. I'm certainly not staying on here until my house is sold. I can't tell you how much I long to get out of this ghastly village.'

It gave me a feeling of panic to hear that Mrs Butterhorn was leaving. She was Cressida's only close neighbour. Once she left, my wife would feel even more isolated and threatened.

'What will you do in London?' I asked her. 'What sort of life are you planning to lead there?'

'I'm not going to find it easy,' she said. 'But then life has never been easy for me. My mother was a great beauty. You needn't look so astonished . . . I promise you, my mother was quite famous for her beauty. She was a dancer. Father was an ugly toad-like man. But he helped her with her career and that may have been why mother liked him. As you can imagine, my appearance was quite an embarrassment to someone like her. Poor woman, she found it hard to accept me. This gave me quite a bad complex. When I was young, I suffered horribly knowing I never could be beautiful . . . Eventually I tried to find a way to get round that . . . I had the dream that I could be someone who *did* things that were beautiful. That's where the passion for gardening started . . . Even when I was married to Mervyn I tried to make his London house look as beautiful as I could. I polished the dining room table. I used to decorate it with lovely cut-glass bowls full of flowers – I did all that sort of thing. It wasn't as creative as making a garden. I often felt frustrated but it was the best I could do. Now I feel my whole dream of doing beautiful things was always rather hopeless. You can only carry it out on such a pathetically small and useless scale . . .'

'It's still worth it.' I didn't know if this was true or if I was merely saying it to cheer up Mrs Butterhorn.

'I must go back and hit the old sack!' She rose to her feet, looking stocky and deceptively masterful in her oilskin jacket and her rubber waders.

'Stay for one more drink,' I begged her. 'I want to ask your advice.'

Mrs Butterhorn deliberated, knitting her tufted grey eyebrows. She then sat down again. 'I won't be able to sleep a wink if I do go home, so there's not much point in rushing back to get my beauty sleep!'

133

I asked her if she would like to spend the night in the cottage. She could have the guest room. I could sleep on the sofa. If she was frightened to be alone in her house, we would be very glad to have her.

A peculiar and embarrassed expression came over her face. She thanked me very much. It was extremely kind but she would be perfectly all right in her own house. There was nothing to be scared of. She had to stop being so foolish.

She is terrified, I thought. Mrs Butterhorn is terrified to sleep in our cottage.

She asked me what advice I wanted her to give me. I told her there was a problem, that I had to return to London very soon because of various work commitments there. Did she feel it would be cruel and irresponsible to leave Cressida and Mary Rose in the country on their own?

Mrs Butterhorn thought for a moment. Her expression was grim. She said that if I was unable to stay with my family in Beckham, I most certainly ought to take them up to London. In her opinion it would be disastrous if my wife and daughter were to be left alone together in the cottage.

I didn't like to be told this. Cressida and Mary Rose couldn't possible move into my flat in London. That was unthinkable. I wondered whether to tell Mrs Butterhorn that I wanted to divorce Cressida. I was suddenly tempted to confide in her.

Never had my situation seemed so messy and insoluble. There could hardly have been a more unfortunate moment to announce to Cressida that I wanted to leave her for ever. It was ironic that since the conception of Mary Rose, this was the first time that my physical presence had any real value to her.

I felt too fatigued to try to explain all the complications of my unusual marriage to Mrs Butterhorn. I merely told her it would be impractical for me to take Cressida and Mary Rose up to London. I didn't have suitable accommodation. As Cressida suffered from a pathological dislike of cities, I also doubted she would want to come with me. As I said this, I remembered Cressida's face when in the hospital she told me she couldn't bear to bring up a child in London. I saw such a look of genuine anguish and fear in her beautiful glass-like eyes that I realised she was serious about this. For her the city teemed with dark phantasmagoric dangers which were a threat to the life of her beloved child. I could have mocked her absurd contention and insisted that many thousands of children routinely were brought up in London and to all appearances escaped the evils of the city unscathed. It hadn't suited me to fight her on this issue. I was relieved that she insisted on living in the country.

It seemed to anger Mrs Butterhorn when I tried to explain that Cressida had an exaggerated horror of bringing up Mary Rose in any city. She admitted that she herself had never liked London, but only because she disliked noise and pollution. She certainly never saw it as a sink of corruption and depravity. It was grotesque for my wife to pretend Mary Rose would be harmed by being moved to the city. How could it be any more unhealthy than letting the wretched child remain in Beckham?

'That little girl must not be left alone with your wife in that cottage. I can't tell you how violently I feel about that!' Mrs Butterhorn had suddenly started to boom again and she used the tone with which she addressed Crake, her arthritic old gardener.

I assured her that I would not leave them alone. If I myself was unable to stay with them, I would arrange for someone else to come to the cottage.

'I don't want to meddle,' Mrs Butterhorn said. 'I barely know you. So it may seem impertinent if I tell you what I think. But you asked my advice and maybe you need a stranger to tell you where your duty lies. You are playing the ostrich . . . In your heart of hearts you must know just as well as I do that your wife is unfit to be in charge of that little girl. I therefore beg you as that unfortunate child's father to arrange for her to be removed from that woman's care.'

'You can't be saying that I ought to take Mary Rose away from Cressida?' Mrs Butterhorn had really succeeded in shocking me. I reacted as if she had urged me to cut off Cressida's head. How could I possibly remove Mary Rose from her mother? The suggestion was farcical. Where would the child live? Did Mrs Butterhorn expect me to take care of her?

I told her that I found her advice outrageous. I was surprised that she could suggest that I do anything quite so cruel to Cressida. Hadn't Mrs Butterhorn realised that my wife's entire existence centred round Mary Rose? She worshipped her. If anyone were to try to take Mary Rose from her, she would be destroyed. I reminded Mrs Butterhorn that apart from any emotional considerations, legally I was in no position to remove Mary Rose from her mother's care. Cressida had not battered the child. She had not been negligent. On what legal grounds could I claim that my wife was incompetent as a mother? I admitted that I thought my wife was misguided in the way she wanted to make my daughter aware of all the gruesome aspects of the murder of little Maureen Sutton. I agreed with Mrs Butterhorn that I found this disturbing. However, I felt we should try to be fair to my wife. The case had obviously traumatised her. She was living in a state of terror and therefore could be forgiven if her behaviour at times was not quite as balanced as one might wish. Once the police found the man who'd attacked the little Sutton girl, she would no longer feel that her daughter was at risk and she would regain her old serenity and be once again a calm and loving mother to Mary Rose.

Mrs Butterhorn listened to my speech in silence. She looked utterly disgusted.

'I'd like to ask you something,' she said. 'Has it occurred to you that the police may not find the killer for many weeks, even months? They may never find him. Have you thought of that? I think you should remember that many crimes go unsolved . . .'

Mrs Butterhorn got to her feet and thanked me for the brandy. 'I can't make you take action,' she said. 'But think about my advice. If some tragedy occurs in that cottage because you were too weak and lazy to listen to me, you will have to hold yourself responsible.'

As she waddled out through the door of the Red Lion, a feeling of despair came over me. I wanted to rush after her and say that I was going to take her advice. But I couldn't bring myself to do it. I ordered myself one last whisky because everything in my life seemed so hopeless I was frightened I might start to cry.

Chapter Eleven

I didn't see any police cars on my drive back to the cottage. The moon was out and it was very still. I found I couldn't resist taking a quick glance at the woods next to the council estate. They looked like an ominous wall of blackness against the streaky acid white of the moonlit sky. Having seen their dark formation I quickly returned my eyes to the road. I felt guilty, as if by looking at those trees I'd committed an obscenity.

I suddenly saw the shadowy figure of a man walking by the side of the Beckham green and my heart started pounding. When I drove up to him, I saw it was Tom Crake, Mrs Butterhorn's gardener. I wondered why he was out so late and what he was doing. I then realised this was outrageous. The poor man had a perfect right to be walking round the green if he chose to, and in point of fact it wasn't very late. There was no reason to expect every inhabitant of Beckham to remain permanently indoors because a child had met her death in the local woods.

As my headlights shone on him, Tom Crake turned his head towards my car. I saw his gnarled old face. It had an expression of animal-like terror. He in his turn wondered why I was driving around alone. As Mrs Butterhorn had said, the atmosphere in this village was unspeakable.

All the lights were on when I arrived at the cottage. When I knocked, Cressida took such a long time to answer I wondered if she had gone to sleep. Finally, however, she came to the door and having examined me through the peephole, she unlocked all the bolts.

'You promised you wouldn't stay long in the pub,' she said accusingly. I apologised. But I felt the mutual politeness that had sustained us in the past was soon going to wear very thin.

As I went into the living room, to my horror I noticed there was a framed photograph on the mantelpiece. It was a large picture of the grinning little Maureen Sutton. My wife had cut it out of some newspaper. The sight of the child's cheery face filled me with anger, although I would have found it hard to explain why it enraged me so much. I wanted to take the photograph and hurl it into the fire.

'I've just heard the news on the radio,' Cressida said. 'They still haven't found him.'

I didn't answer her. I was feeling too infuriated by the sight of the photograph.

'I went up to the woods the other day,' she said.

'I know you did. I just met Mrs Butterhorn in the pub and she told me.'

'I took Mary Rose to see the place where it happened.'

'Mrs Butterhorn told me that too. I find it quite disgusting.'

'I don't want Mary Rose to be shielded.'

'That's all too horribly obvious.' My voice was choked. I found it hard to speak.

'I want Mary Rose to know every vile thing that man did to that other child! I want to make it vivid to her so that she never forgets what men can do to her . . . Maureen Sutton was probably shielded. If the poor little creature hadn't been allowed to be so innocent and trusting, she might still be with us today . . .'

As Cressida spoke, she kept smiling in the unnerving way that Mrs Butterhorn had described to me. Her smiles weren't proper smiles. They seemed more like terrible nervous tics.

Feeling too sickened to make any comment on what she'd told me, I went next door into the kitchen to make myself some tea.

As I put on the kettle, I noticed that the awful steel

139

cauldron in which my wife always boiled our sheets was on the stove. It was full to the brim with some kind of obnoxious black liquid.

'What on earth is all this black muck?' I asked her when she followed me into the kitchen.

'It's dye.'

'Dye?'

'Yes, dye. I've been dyeing Mary Rose's clothes.'

'Why for the love of God have you been doing that?'

'I've dyed them for the funeral.'

'What funeral are you talking about?' I appeared slow-witted. I couldn't face what I knew she was going to tell me.

'It's the funeral tomorrow. It's the funeral of that poor little child.'

I suddenly wanted to run out of the cottage, to go next door and wake up Mrs Butterhorn and ask her to come round. I needed her bossy voice and her air of masculine authority. To all outward appearances she was tough and hard-headed and I felt these qualities were needed if my wife was to be brought to her senses.

'You can't be taking Mary Rose to that funeral. You must be joking.'

Cressida gave me an odd and defiant look. I remembered Mrs Butterhorn's description of my wife's 'snake-pit' expression.

'Of course I'm taking her.'

'But you can't do that,' I protested. 'You never knew the child. It's obscene and ghoulish for you to go. You've never met the Suttons. They won't want you there. If you turn up at the graveside, they'll find it an outrageous intrusion. I imagine that any family that has just sustained a tragedy of such an appalling nature would want to be left alone with their grief.'

'I think the Suttons will want me to be there,' Cressida said stubbornly.

'How could they want you there? How could they want Mary Rose? How could they want two strangers?'

140

'They won't feel we are strangers,' Cressida said to me, and I'd never seen her look so crazy. 'Shall I tell you why the Sutton's won't feel that? Because they'll know that Mary Rose and I are the only people in the world who care just as much as they do that their poor little child was murdered by some fucking bestial man!'

Chapter Twelve

After Cressida told me why she was taking my daughter to the Sutton funeral, I went up to bed. I was so dumbfounded by her uncharacteristic vulgarity I couldn't think of anything else to say to her.

I went up the ladder staircase and at the end of the narrow little creaky landing, I saw the door of my daughter's bedroom. Cressida had put a huge black bolt on it so the child could be locked inside. There was not a sound coming from the bedroom. I wondered if Mary Rose was sleeping. I had the suspicion she was lying there awake.

I wondered if I ought to go in and see her. I didn't know how to behave if I did pay her a visit. Would it be appropriate to play the hearty loving father, to give her a playful tickle and a bear hug? I never went into my daughter's bedroom. Now I was frightened to do so as if, behind the bolted door of her bedroom, I was terrified of what I might see.

The bed had not been made in the guest room. The ash tray was filled with the stubs of the cigarettes I'd smoked the last time I had stayed in the cottage.

Most of the night I stayed awake, staring at the oppressive black beam that slanted down from the ceiling. It was as if I was hoping it would tell me what I ought to do.

I was certain of only one thing. I couldn't stay on in this cottage. I knew the limits of my own nervous tolerance and was convinced my sanity would snap if I stayed for long in this terrible little period house with Cressida talking of nothing but the murder in the woods and thinking every time a bough snapped in the garden it was the footstep of an approaching killer.

Yet I knew that someone ought to stay with her. She was already in such a peculiar hyper-agitated state that if she had many more nights of sleeplessness and terror, I feared she might become totally deranged.

I wondered if I ought to offer to take her up to London and find her and Mary Rose a room in a hotel. Would her fear of the Beckham rapist be stronger than her neurotic conviction that some intrinsic danger would be done to Mary Rose if she was brought up in the city? But even if she agreed to move to a London hotel with the child, it would not be feasible economically for them both to stay there for very long. As Mrs Butterhorn had pointed out, I chose to pretend my wife's crisis was a temporary one that would abate the moment the police found the Beckham killer, whereas there was in fact no guarantee they would ever find him at all.

I thrashed around in my bed trying to think of any solution. Maybe I ought to persuade Cressida to sell the Beckham cottage and find herself another one in a different part of the country. But even if she agreed, that would take time and would not solve the problem that she was in no condition to be left alone in the immediate future.

Neither did it solve the far greater problem, the problem that seemed so monumental that I could hardly bear to think about it. Mary Rose quite obviously should be removed from my wife's care. My daughter would sustain incalculable psychological injuries if she was allowed to remain with a woman whose maternal sense had become so distorted that her only concern was to plunge the child into the morass of her own ugly and paranoid fantasies. Mrs Butterhorn was right. But how was I going to remove Mary Rose?

Mrs Butterhorn had warned me that she believed some tragedy might occur in the cottage if I was too weak and lazy to take Mary Rose away from Cressida. And although I could have scoffed at this idea and dismissed it as over-dramatic and hysterical, I took her warning seriously and it never left my mind. Lying staring at the black beam in the guest room, I felt overwhelmed by a sense of impending catastrophe. This feeling was made all the more dreadful by the fact I lacked any notion of the form the disaster I feared might take.

In the morning I resolved to talk to Mrs Butterhorn and tell her I now shared her conviction that Mary Rose should be removed as soon as possible from her mother. I would also point out to her that having made this difficult decision, there were many practical questions as to how this should be accomplished. I couldn't see myself calmly telling Cressida that I not only wanted a divorce but I also wanted Mary Rose. That would be unthinkable.

Obviously I couldn't kidnap the child. My wife would immediately apply for a court order to demand her return and all the police in the country would start searching for me.

If I were to try to take the child away from her mother, it would be inadvisable to use gangster tactics. It had to be done legally. But even if I obtained a legal separation from Cressida, I doubted that my chances of obtaining custody would be very strong. It was unlikely that any court would see me as fit to take charge of a small girl. Only if Cressida were declared mentally ill would I have a chance of gaining custody of Mary Rose, and although Cressida's recent behaviour had been unpleasant and eccentric, it was doubtful any doctor would certify her as insane.

I assumed Mrs Butterhorn would advise me immediately to go to London in order to consult a lawyer and find out my exact position. But before I left Beckham, I felt it was my duty to find someone to sleep in the cottage in my absence. It had to be someone I knew very well. In a crazy flash I thought of Gloria. I then came to my senses and realised the idea was grotesque. Why would Gloria, who no longer wished ever to see me again, agree to stay with my wife?

This ridiculous idea was followed by another almost equally foolish. I thought of asking my mother to help me. Since my father's death she had remarried and now lived in Paris with her new husband, who was a jeweller. When I thought about it more rationally, I realised that as I'd had little contact with my mother in recent years, she would be flabbergasted if I suddenly telephoned her and asked her to fly over to England and move into a cottage in Kent with a daughter-in-law and a grandchild she had not known existed.

I then tried to find a less preposterous solution. Tom Crake and his sister? If I bribed them both, could I persuade them to move in with Cressida? Though this idea was not as far-fetched as my previous ones, when I examined it closely it didn't seem very satisfactory. If Tom Crake's sister was as neurasthenic as I'd been led to believe and herself lived in mortal terror of the rapist, she would hardly be the ideal companion for Cressida. Most likely she would work my wife up and inflame all her worst fears. Then old Tom Crake might find he couldn't tolerate the combined hysteria of these two nerve-wrung women.

Just as I despaired that I would ever think of anyone who would be prepared to sleep in the cottage, I thought of Fay Wisherton. In the last few years she had been working for me regularly as a typist. She came several times a week to my flat in order to deal with my bills, my correspondence and my income tax.

Fay Wisherton was a young woman who was chiefly remarkable for the neutrality of her colouring. Almost everything about her was beige. She had beige hair, a beige skin and fawn-coloured eyes which were fringed with beige eyelashes. In her dress she avoided flamboyance. Her suits and her shoes and all her other accessories were equally subdued and her favourite shade seemed to be a pale discreet tan. As a personality Fay Wisherton was helpful and soothing. She was a noiseless tactful presence and allowed one to forget she was in the room. Gloria was convinced that in her subtle and ladylike way Fay Wishterton was secretly in love with me.

I never felt Gloria was right. Fay exuded a faint aura of regret and sadness. But I felt that if she nursed a sorrow, it came from something that had happened in the past rather than anything she was experiencing in the present. Maybe she had had some unhappy love affair, or even marriage. All I knew was that she would never dream of discussing her personal affairs and they always would remain a mystery because of her reticence and discretion.

The more I thought about it, the more I was convinced she could be persuaded to stay a few nights in the cottage. She would be astonished to learn I had a wife and child as she had always seen me with Gloria. But with her tact she would quickly disguise her amazement. There was every hope she would agree to do what I asked her with her usual unruffled willingness. I felt her serene presence might help to dampen Cressida's nervous excitability. I was so relieved to have had the idea of inviting Fay Wisherton to keep my wife company that in the small hours of the morning I finally got some sleep.

Chapter Thirteen

In the morning when I woke, Mary Rose and Cressida were both in the bathroom. I heard sounds of running water. My wife was talking to my daughter. Her tone was low and excited. I couldn't hear what she was saying.

I went downstairs to the kitchen, which looked neglected and squalid. Dirty dishes were piled high in the sink. The great cauldron of dye was still on the stove. I was troubed by the untidiness because it suggested that psychologically Cressida had ceased to inhabit her dream Tudor cottage. It was as if at the moment her only true home was the Beckham woods where they'd found the multilated little corpse of Maureen Sutton.

I couldn't find any coffee. Cressida had not bothered to go shopping or to order any provisions. I searched the empty larder and was glad to find a tea-bag.

Upstairs I heard the creak of floor boards. There were whispers and the muffled sounds of excited preparation and conspiratorial activity. My wife and Mary Rose were getting ready for the funeral.

Finally they came down the ladder staircase. Both of them were dressed in deepest mourning. They looked like figures in a Greek tragedy. Cressida had found herself some kind of heavy veil that fell to her waist and completely obscured her face. Mary Rose was wearing a black blouse and black gymslip. Even her socks were black because her mother had dyed them in the cauldron.

As I watched them descend, their appearance struck me as hilarious rather than moving. Yet my desire to laugh was purely nervous.

Mary Rose looked even worse than I'd feared she might. In the last week she'd become so thin she looked anorexic. She was ashen pale and the mauve patches under her eyes had turned the colour of cement. She wore a black headscarf. Somehow she no longer looked like a child. She seemed more like a miniature verson of an old and unhappy woman.

She flinched when she saw me in the kitchen. It was if she expected me to strike her. She cowered away and clung to the black skirt of her mother.

Cressida made her a cup of weak tea with a tea-bag. There was something infuriating in the way she kept her great black veil down in the kitchen. I couldn't understand how she managed to see through it and I was frightened she was going to burn herself as she poured out boiling water from the kettle.

'We are off now!' she announced. Her manner and tone were exalted. I found that inappropriate.

'Aren't you going to give Mary Rose anything to eat before she goes?' I asked. It was a horrible damp morning and it shocked me that my daughter was being forced to go off to this awful funeral on an empty stomach.

'Mary Rose doesn't feel hungry at a time like this any more than I do . . . I shouldn't imagine that at this moment the Suttons are sitting down to enjoy a large breakfast.'

She helped Mary Rose into her newly dyed black coat and unlocked the bolts on the front door and off she went with my daughter trailing behind her.

From a window I watched them as they walked off to Maureen Sutton's funeral. As I watched the big black figure being followed like a duck by a pathetically small black duckling, I felt quite certain that Mrs Butterhorn was right when she said Mary Rose should be removed from Cressida's care. I also felt she was only correct theoretically.

I saw Cressida as poisonous that morning. Mary Rose

had been bred from this woman's poisons and presumably she was immune to them for they were part of her. If she were to be severed from the poisonous source that had always nurtured her, I was uncertain that the child could survive.

Once Cressida and Mary Rose had disappeared out of sight, I telephoned Fay Wisherton and warned her I wanted to make an unusual request. I didn't think she had realised I was married but in fact I had a wife and child who lived in Kent. I promised I would explain to her later why I'd kept their existence secret.

I went on to say that I was staying with my wife at this moment in a village called Beckham. No doubt she had read in the papers that recently there had been an exceptionally nasty child rape and killing in the area. Quite naturally this had made my wife feel nervous. Until the killer was arrested, she hated to be alone at night . . .

I kept talking very quickly, hoping the speed of my delivery would prevent Fay Wisherton from realising that the request I was making was outlandish.

I told her that unfortunately I had various urgent commitments which compelled me to return to London. Could she possibly come down to stay with my wife in my absence? Naturally I would pay her by the hour as if she was carrying out a secretarial assignment. She would be doing me a great favour if she accepted . . .

Fay Wisherton was silent for a moment. She was clearly stunned but in a different, more delicate way than the average person would have been. She gave a nervous cough, just a quiver of sound.

'And when were you hoping that I would come down to stay with your wife?'

'Tonight. If that doesn't upset your plans.'

'And you say there is a rapist at large in the neighbourhood?'

Under Fay Wisherton's bland and reassuring tones, for

the first time since I'd met her, I detected a faint note of hysteria.

'I assure you there is no danger. We've got every sort of bar and bolt on the cottage. It's as well-defended as Fort Knox. As you can imagine the whole village is blue with police . . . I only want someone to be with my wife in order to give her moral support. When she's alone at night, the killing preys on her mind . . .'

Fay Wisherton still sounded hesitant. 'There's no way you could arrange to stay on with your wife yourself?'

'No way at all,' I lied quickly.

'Well . . . I suppose I could go down to Kent tonight. But I haven't got anyone to take care of my cat.'

'Can't you take the cat with you?'

'Oh no. I really wouldn't like to do that.'

'My wife would be delighted if you brought it. She's very fond of animals.'

'It's not that. I wouldn't like to take my cat to the country.'

'But your cat would probably like the country.' I was getting desperate. The situation was unbearable. Fay Wisherton was willing to come down and stay with Cressida. But now there was this problem of her boring cat.

'I'm frightened my cat might be chased by dogs if I took her to the country.'

'I'll take your cat.' Now I've really gone insane, I thought. I hate cats. I can hardly be in the same room as a cat. But I'm willing to take Fay Wisherton's horrible animal if by so doing I can avoid spending another night in the same house as Cressida. And yet it's all so hopeless. Even if I manage to inveigle Fay Wisherton to Kent. She will stay one night, maybe two. But what will happen after that? I can hardly expect poor Fay Wisherton to take up permanent residence in Beckham and act as Cressida's life-long bodyguard. When Fay Wisherton returns to London, Cressida's frame of mind is unlikely to be any more stable than it is at present. I shall not be any more keen to stay with her than I am at this moment. Yet I shall still be plagued by the feeling that something awful may happen if Mary Rose and her mother are left on their own.

All the same, Fay Wisherton could provide a short-term solution to my problem and that seemed much better than nothing. As I couldn't see any long-term solution, I felt the only thing was to do the best that I could day by day.

I told Fay Wisherton that when I got to London in the afternoon, I would come round and collect her cat. She could then take the train to Beckham so that Cressida would have someone with her by the time it got dark.

'What sort of person is your wife? I hope you don't think it's rude me asking. But I shall be in rather a peculiar position staying with a woman I've never met. I'd just like you to tell me a little bit about her. I hope you don't mind . . .'

Poor Fay Wisherton. She had a perfect right to ask what Cressida was like. She was going to be shut up alone with her in the cottage. Yet she sounded desperately worried that she had overstepped the bounds of good taste.

I found her question hard to answer. Should I tell her what Cressida had once been like? Should I say she was a domestic, maternal type? When Fay Wisherton saw the state of the cottage, when she heard that my wife had dragged Mary Rose off to the funeral, wouldn't she wonder if I'd gone out of my mind?

I didn't want to lie to Fay Wisherton but I feared that if I gave her my truthful impression of what Cressida was like at the moment, she would refuse to come down to the cottage. I therefore made a dithering attempt to describe Cressida in phrases which were not strictly dishonest although they gave no accurate picture of her personality. I said she was country-loving. Although this was true, it was not quite as healthy and normal as it sounded. She was country-loving but only in a negative sense because of her phobia that Mary Rose would come to harm in any city.

I said she was shy. This too was only a half-truth. She

151

might seem to be shy because her life was reclusive. But I often thought that Cressida had no friends because she was arrogant rather than timid. It was as if she felt no one in the world was worth bothering about apart from herself and Mary Rose.

As I tried to give an attractive description of my wife it struck me I was fortunate that Fay Wisherton hadn't asked me what my wife's interests were. It would be difficult to explain to a stranger that the rape of Maureen Sutton was now the only thing that Cressida thought or cared about. It was as if it had invaded her brain, driving out all other concerns.

I had such a violent longing to be able to escape with a good conscience from the cottage that I knew there was a certain ruthlessness in the way I was forcing the unfortunate Fay Wisherton to become Cressida's companion without troubling whether she would find this companionship agreeable. I felt guilty about this and therefore tried to persuade myself that Fay Wisherton, as a detached stranger, would be able to view Cressida's peculiarities with much more compassion than I could muster.

My relationship with my wife had always been cruel and complicated. It was therefore possible that my whole impression of her was unfair and distorted. I saw the frenzy with which Cressida was reacting to the rape as demented and ugly. Maybe Fay Wisherton, as a woman, would take a different view and find it understandable. Quite possibly she would find my wife likable and they could become friends. I said all this to myself because I hated to think that I was luring the unsuspecting and pleasant Miss Wisherton into a situation which she might find very disagreeable indeed.

Chapter Fourteen

Once I'd arranged for Fay Wisherton to come down to
Beckham, I wandered about feeling restless and miserable in the cottage. It was freezing cold. Cressida no
longer went off to the woods to collect logs. When I went
into the living room I was upset by the face of Maureen
Sutton on the mantelpiece. She was being buried right at
this moment. The horror of what had happened to her
struck me properly for the first time. All the women I
knew had had an immediate and direct response to her
killing. Mine was delayed as if on some emotional level I'd
refused to react. Looking at the photograph of the little
girl, I was overwhelmed by a surge of violent feelings
which manifested themselves physically. I went hot. I
went cold. I thought I was going to vomit.

I decided that I'd go next door and talk to Mrs Butterhorn. After that I'd set off for London. I was anxious to
be gone before Cressida and Mary Rose got back. I
dreaded hearing my wife's description of the funeral.

When I rang her bell, Mrs Butterhorn came to the door
looking exhausted and distraught. She invited me in for
coffee. The disorder of her house no longer shocked me as
much as it had in the past. My own cottage was now every
bit as slovenly and uncared for. Mrs Butterhorn at least
had lit a fire.

She told me that once again she'd not slept all night.
She'd been foolish when she'd refused my invitation to
sleep in our cottage.

'I wasn't exactly frightened that the killer might break

153

in. It was more ghastly than that. I lay in bed feeling frightened of everything . . .'

She clumped about in her kitchen and made me coffee and poured it into what looked to me like a dangerously dirty cup.

'How's your wife today. How's your little girl?'

'I don't know what to do about them, Mrs Butterhorn.'

She tossed her grey hair impatiently. With irritable gestures she tipped slops into an overfilled rubbish bin and threw bones to her various yelping dogs.

'I'm afraid I really can't help you,' she said brusquely. 'I said everything there is to be said on that subject yesterday when we spoke in the pub. Maybe I went too far . . . I told you I'm convinced that your wife is having a very destructive effect on your little daughter. If you don't care to do anything about it, that's your business. I'm not going to say any more . . .'

'Mrs Butterhorn . . .' I protested. 'I've just spent the night in the cottage and I now think everything you say is true. You are wrong that I'm not prepared to try to do anything about it. I'm going up to London today to consult a solicitor about a divorce.

Mrs Butterhorn looked at me with much more sympathy.

'So it's as bad as that? You really want to divorce her?'

'Oh, I've wanted to divorce her for a long time. But if I try to take custody of my daughter, that is a much more serious step. I confess the idea of it terrifies me. I don't think I'd be at all good at bringing up Mary Rose. I wouldn't understand her needs.'

'Why do you think your wife is receptive to your daughter's needs?' Mrs Butterhorn asked me. 'The last time I saw the child, she looked like a total wreck.'

I then told her that Cressida had taken Mary Rose to the funeral of Maureen Sutton. Her reaction was more violent than I'd expected. Never had she looked more toad-like. Her face seemed to swell with rage. She said she'd never heard of anything so appalling. I should have

154

prevented it. Why was I so passive and hopeless? What would Mary Rose feel when she saw the little coffin of the other child? Surely I could see how gratuitously cruel the whole thing was. I really made her angry . . .

I tried to explain that unless I'd knocked Cressida unconscious, I saw no way that I could have stopped my wife from taking Mary Rose to the funeral. Mrs Butterhorn clearly didn't believe this. She continued to look extremely annoyed with me.

In order to change the subject, I told her my secretary would be coming down to stay in the cottage when I went to London. I asked Mrs Butterhorn to do me a favour. Would she invite Fay Wisherton to tea? My secretary had never met my wife and I didn't know if they would get on. I'd like to feel there was someone who would be nice to her in case she found her stay in the cottage a strain.

Mrs Butterhorn promised to ask her to tea. At that moment there was a knock. We both jumped. Our nerves were raw. Could Cressida have come back from the funeral? Mrs Butterhorn opened the door to an old woman who was nearly bald except for a few wisps of hair which she had dyed bright red. This ancient figure was crying pitifully. Mrs Butterhorn took her by the arm and helped her into the house. She sat her down on the sofa, where the old woman continued to weep. It was a long time until she managed to control herself enough to speak. Finally she asked if she could see Mrs Butterhorn alone.

I tactfully got up and left. I went back to the cottage. I wondered what could have caused the old woman's terrible grief. I'd rarely seen a person in such acute distress.

I decided I would set off for London immediately. I was haunted by the image of the old woman's semi-bald head bobbing with each sob as she exploded with grief on Mrs Butterhorn's sofa. It had made me keener than ever to escape from Beckham, where everyone seemed so miserable. I left a note for Cressida explaining that something unforeseen had come up and I was obliged to return to the city. I'd arranged for my secretary Miss Wisherton to come to the cottage to keep her company so she need not be frightened at night. Miss Wisherton was very nice and I hoped she would like her.

As I left the cottage and was walking towards my car, I saw Mrs Butterhorn rushing through the wicker gate that led from her garden. That morning she was not wearing her trawler outfit; she was dressed in khaki battledress from the army surplus store. There was something frantic about the speed with which she was approaching me. She looked like a stocky old soldier fleeing from some military disaster. I couldn't tell if she was laughing or crying. But her face was contorted and excitement had turned it maroon.

'Something petrifying has happened!' she gasped as she came up to me.

'What has happened?' My immediate thought was that something devastating must have happened to Mary Rose.

'You saw that old woman who just arrived at my house in tears?'

'I saw she was in a terrible state.'

'And with good reason. You can't believe what she's just told me.'

'Who is that old woman?'

'Eliza Crake. Tom Crake's sister.'

'What did she tell you?'

'It's so awful I hardly like to repeat it.'

'Please . . . Mrs Butterhorn. Please try to pull yourself together.'

Her eyes were bulging more than usual. She looked like a terrified Pekinese.

'Tom Crake has confessed!'

'Oh my God!'

'Exactly,' Mrs Butterhorn whispered.

'When did he confess?'

'Early this morning. He went down to the police station on his own.'

'God Almighty!'

156

'Exactly.'

'Do you want to come into my cottage? This must have been quite a shock to you.'

She refused. She ought to get back to Eliza Crake. She was very worried about her. The poor old creature hadn't stopped crying since her brother told her what he'd done. Mrs Butterhorn felt she ought to be made to see a doctor. A shock like this might have a disastrous effect on her heart.

'Shall I come and see her?' I asked.

Mrs Butterhorn shook her head. She didn't think Eliza Crake could bear to see anyone at this moment. The poor old woman said she didn't know how she was going to survive the disgrace. Yet she hadn't minded Mrs Butterhorn coming over to tell me the dreadful news. She had said there was no point in minding. Everyone was going to know soon enough anyway. At any moment it would be a headline in the national newspapers.

'It's pathetic,' Mrs Butterhorn said. 'Eliza Crake keeps saying she knows that old Tom couldn't have done it. She says he's not the sort of man who could ever do a thing like that . . .'

'Did she see him the night that it happened?'

'Yes, she did. She cooked him sausages when he got home that evening. She says it makes her sick to think of him sitting in her kitchen eating sausages . . .'

I told Mrs Butterhorn to go back and get a doctor for Eliza Crake. I would telephone her once I got to London and find out if there was any more news.

Once she had gone back to her house, I got into my car and set off for London. As I drove towards the city I tried to digest the news. The more I thought about it the more I found it incredible. The killer was no longer at lärge. Previously he'd seemed such a phantom-like figure of unfathomable evil that it seemed an anticlimax he'd turned out to be someone as familiar as Tom Crake. It was as if too simple an answer had been given to a puzzle that had once seemed so infinitely complex as to be insoluble.

And yet that wasn't true. For I also found the fact that I knew him horrifying. So many questions were posed. Had the old gardener planned this crime for a long time? Was he always dreaming of it maniacally as he pottered round Mrs Butterhorn's garden pruning her roses while she showered him with her booming upper-class abuse? Was there a point when all the anger and frustrated lust that had seethed for years inside that diseased old arthritic body at last could only find outlet by destroying someone who was healthy and young?

And what had made that old man set off for the police station? Was it a monumental guilt that hoped to find expiation by punishment or had he simply found the feeling of being perpetually hunted insufferable? I remembered the terror when I passed him the day before on the green. No wonder he had looked at me with that expression of agony.

How well did he remember what he'd done to that child in the woods? Was the whole episode clearly etched in his memory or was it shrouded? Had it taken on the aspects of a dark and ill-remembered dream? Did he feel unconnected with the savagery of his own actions so that though he confessed he felt all the time removed, as if he was confessing to a crime committed by someone else?

And how would Cressida react when she heard Tom Crake was the killer? Surely she'd be glad to hear Maureen Sutton's murderer was in custody. She would now no longer need to make my daughter keep guard at night. There would now be no reason for her to feel that the same brutal creature who had ravaged Maureen Sutton was stalking round outside the cottage hoping to get his hands on Mary Rose.

All the same I suspected that she would only find the bombshell news reassuring on one level. She might well feel shattered by the information that a man as seemingly harmless as old Tom Crake had been capable of committing this atrocity. Cressida with her dream of isolating her beloved little daughter from all the poisons of an evil infested universe could hardly enjoy the notion that ever since she'd lived in the cottage, Tom Crake had been limping around in the next door garden.

A nightmarish thought then occurred to me. I'd seriously considered bribing Tom Crake to stay in the cottage with Cressida. What would have happened if I'd moved that rheumatic old rapist into the same house as my little daughter? It didn't bear thinking about. And even if the old man had done nothing worse than go off to the police station to confess while he was living under the same roof as Mary Rose, that situation alone would probably have been enough to send Cressida right out of her mind.

As it was now, I foresaw that Cressida would most likely become hysterical when she was informed of the gardener's confession. I was glad that Fay Wisherton would be with her rather than myself.

But once Cressida's inevitable hysteria had subsided, surely her state of mind would improve. I found myself feeling optimistic. Surely there was every hope that once she knew the slayer of Maureen Sutton was behind bars, she would regain her serenity and I would no longer feel that in her paranoid dementia she was doing incalculable psychological harm to Mary Rose.

The realisation that Tom Crake by his early confession had spared me from any obligation to try to take custody of my daughter was such a relief that it sent me into a mood of euphoria. Until the threat was removed, I had not dared to admit how much I'd dreaded the idea of bringing up Mary Rose on my own. I didn't want that whey-faced little girl with the forlorn eyes sitting in my flat. What would she do there except miss her mother?

I'd tried to persuade myself that if I embarked on a legal battle with Cressida, there was little likelihood that I could ever win custody of Mary Rose. But I'd sometimes had the fear that if I exerted enough financial pressure on my wife, there was the horrendous possibility that I might be successful. I would have used squalid and cruel tactics to gain something I prayed to lose.

But I no longer had to think about all this. The crisis was over. Cressida could settle down and resume with her child the humdrum existence she had led before the killing. This made me feel so happy that when on my arrival in London I drove to Miss Wisherton's flat I hardly minded taking her cat.

Miss Wisherton had already packed and she was ready to set off for Beckham. I could have guessed that her suitcase would be beige.

Her cat was called Tabby. Her cat was beige as well. It was a big fat creature. To me it looked overfed and spoilt. She gave me a lot of instructions as to its ways, when to give it milk and when to abstain. She had written me a list of the various cat foods it liked. Apparently it suffered from a fear of dogs. I assured her there were none in my building and her bland face looked relieved.

I had already decided not to tell her that the Beast of Beckham had been found. She would feel that if the police were holding the killer there was no longer any reason for her to go down to Kent. And I felt that it was still important that she go. It seemed to me vital that Cressida should be with someone calm and sensible when she first heard the news that Tom Crake had raped and taken the life of Maureen Sutton.

I gave Fay Wisherton the number of a taxi service that she could ring on her arrival at the Beckham station. She said that she was very grateful to have it as she had been frightened that I would expect her to walk to the cottage.

She gave an embarrassed little tinkle of a laugh. 'You'll think me very silly but I don't want to walk anywhere in that village. Not after having read the account of the rape in the papers.'

I assured her she wouldn't have to walk. I was startled that a young woman as seemingly solid and sensible as Fay Wisherton should be manifesting signs of the same irrational terror over this incident as all the other women I knew. It was an atavistic female fear that I had to respect because it existed, yet it was one that I could only partially understand. The odds against my secretary being raped if she walked in broad daylight from the railway station to the cottage through the police patrolled lanes of Beckham were, in my opinion, very large indeed.

Once again I thanked Fay Wisherton for her kindness in agreeing to keep my wife company. I picked up her cat and its cumbersome and smelly basket which was full of hairs. I was convinced from the first sight of it that it would give me asthma. I left Fay and drove Tabby and her health-hazardous bedding round to my own flat.

Although it was a delight not to be in the cottage, I nevertheless felt depressed once I got home. Gloria's clothes were still in the wardrobe. I wondered when she would come and collect them. In order to prevent myself from thinking about her, I telephoned a friend and asked him to meet me for lunch. I had first met Mark Egerton when I was at Cambridge. He was now a film director and spent a lot of time in Hollywood. We met in an oyster bar in the West End. Mark had just been in Australia where he had been shooting a film. The film sounded rather awful – some kind of sentimental saga about a family of immigrant settlers – but he was amusing describing the vicissitudes he had endured when he was on location. He was also interesting describing the Australian attitude towards the 'Limey'. We drank a lot of wine and he told me about his life in California. He was entertaining and witty and all his observations were sharp. He asked me about the book I was writing and as I described my project I found my old excitement starting to revive, and I was anxious to get back to work.

I left the lunch feeling more buoyant than I had for a long time. When I tried to analyse why I'd enjoyed the meal so much I decided it was not only because of Mark's company – it was also because there had been no mention of little Maureen Sutton. It had been pure relief to meet someone who didn't feel that her killing was an event so major that it dwarfed all other world catastrophies.

Once I got back to my flat I started to work. Fay Wisherton's cat kept slinking around my study mewing, which I found intensely disturbing. I controlled the anger this fat beige animal aroused in me by reminding myself that I ought to feel grateful to it. If it hadn't been for this disruptive cat with the malevolent amber eyes I would still be in the cottage with Cressida and Mary Rose in their funeral attire, and nothing could be worse than that.

I worked quite well that day despite the unwelcome presence of Tabby. Around six o'clock I started to feel tired and I had a whisky and decided to take a bath. I had the nagging sense that I ought to find out what was happening in Beckham. I wondered if Fay Wisherton had arrived safely, and I also wondered if anyone had told Cressida that Tom Crake was the self-confessed killer, and if they had, how she was adjusting to the fact.

At that moment my telephone rang. It was Mrs Butterhorn. She sounded very excited. She wanted to ask me something important. Could I not tell anyone that Tom Crake had confessed?

'But why keep it a secret?' I asked her. 'It's bound to be in all the newspapers. I haven't seen the *Evening Standard* but they may have the story already for all I know.'

'I'll tell you why you must keep it a secret. Tom Crake didn't do it.'

'But you said he confessed!'

'He did confess. But he still didn't do it.'

'Why on earth did he pretend that he did?'

'God knows,' Mrs Butterhorn said wearily. 'I think we are all going mad in this village.'

She then went on to explain in more detail what had happened. Eliza Crake had been going round the village asking questions in order to find out about her brother's movements the evening that the child disappeared.

Apparently the police had set the time of the killing at around eight o'clock. Tom Crake had been playing darts in a pub in the council estate from six o'clock until about seven. In the pub he had run into a married couple who

162

were selling a lawn-mower. He had left with them around seven and gone to their house to have a look at it. He had stayed on there drinking beer and watching television until about ten o'clock when he'd gone back to his cottage and his sister had cooked him the sausages. The police had checked with all the witnesses who had seen him around the crucial time when the child was abducted. They'd come to the conclusion that it was impossible for him to have taken the child to the woods, for there were too many people who could testify as to his exact movements on that evening. There was another important point in his favour. Some schoolchildren apparently now claimed they had seen Maureen Sutton the evening she was murdered. She was in a black car driven by a man. When asked if she looked frightened they said she'd seemed very happy. She had waved to them as if she wanted to show off that she was being taken for a drive in a car. If the children's testimony turned out to be accurate, it was yet another factor that exonerated Tom Crake from any blame. The old gardener had never learnt to drive. At all events the police, having satisfied themselves that his confession was a false one, had now released him. Eliza Crake was very anxious that no one should know what her brother had done for she felt it was the most shameful thing she'd ever heard of.

All the time Mrs Butterhorn was talking only one thing was going through my mind. If Tom Crake was innocent, as now seemed likely, the killer was still at large. I'd thought my situation had improved but now I realised with horror that it was just as bad as it had ever been. If the rapist was still free Cressida would need someone to stay with her at night.

And then there was the question of her general frame of mind. I'd hoped that once the rapist had been apprehended it would return to normal. But now Tom Crake had turned out to be innocent there was no reason why it might not deteriorate for she would continue to feel that death was waiting for her child behind every bush.

If her mental state deteriorated, then I was once again faced with the awful dilemma as to whether it was my moral duty to do the thing I most dreaded, to try to take Mary Rose out of her mother's care.

I asked Mrs Butterhorn if she knew if Fay Wisherton had arrived at the cottage. Apparently she had. Mrs Butterhorn had seen a fair young woman ringing the bell of the cottage and she had looked very upset for there seemed to be no one to let her in. Mrs Butterhorn had gone over and invited my secretary into her house so that the poor girl could wait in the warm.

'But where on earth was Cressida?' I asked.

'She was still at the funeral.'

'But that's nonsense! She couldn't have still been at the funeral. You know how early she set off this morning.'

'She decided to keep vigil beside the grave of little Maureen Sutton. After the other mourners had left, she stayed on with Mary Rose.'

'But that's ghastly! She must have stayed there for hours.'

'She did,' Mrs Butterhorn said. 'She stayed there most of the day.'

'But Mary Rose must have nearly frozen to death.'

'Evidently the child's teeth were chattering when she came back. She was frozen stiff and was also drenched to the skin. There were heavy showers in Beckham today.'

'Oh God Almighty!' I said. 'What am I going to do?'

'You know perfectly well what I think you ought to do. I don't have to tell you again,' Mrs Butterhorn said.

I asked her if she'd seen Cressida and Mary Rose since they'd got back from the funeral. Apparently she hadn't. It puzzled me how she knew my daughter's teeth were chattering. It appeared that Fay Wisherton had been to her house a second time.

When Cressida had finally returned, Fay Wisherton had gone over to the cottage. About two hours later she had come back to Mrs Butterhorn's house and rung the bell. She had lied to Cressida and said she had left her gloves behind. She used this excuse because she was desperate to talk to Mrs Butterhorn. Various things that my wife had said and done had upset her very much.

'Your poor young secretary was quite shaken up. I really felt very sorry for her. I think you should have warned her what your wife was like. Fay Wisherton seems particularly nice girl.'

I asked her what Cressida had done to distress Fay. It was not encouraging to hear that my secretary was already unhappy. She'd only been with Cressida a few hours. I'd chosen to believe that although my wife had a jarring effect on me she would not have it on everyone.

It appeared that Cressida had given Fay a graphic description of the funeral, which had been small and private and only attended by the dead child's parents and grandparents and couple of close family friends. Cressida had found the service intensely beautiful and moving. As Maureen Sutton's coffin was lowered into the ground, Cressida had made Mary Rose go up to the grave with a bunch of snowdrops which she had thrown on to the small trunk-like box that held the murdered child. When Mrs Sutton saw my daughter approach the grave with the bunch of white flowers, her grief had become uncontrollable. She had started screaming at the top of her voice and her legs collapsed and she had to be physically supported by her relatives.

The thing Fay Wisherton found so terrifying was that Cressida had seemed rather pleased by the devastating effect that Mary Rose's theatrical gesture had on the unfortunate Mrs Sutton. She gave no indication she was aware that it had been an act of cruelty towards the dead child's parents when she produced Mary Rose at this funeral. Fay Wisherton, who was extremely sensitive to the reactions of other people, was convinced that it must have been unbearably painful for the Suttons to see a six-year-old girl in the graveyard at a moment when they were feeling crucified by the loss of their own.

When my wife described the way Mrs Sutton had

broken down she hadn't quite done so with glee but with painstaking attention to detail which suggested she fe some important lesson could be learnt from dwelling o minutiae.

The first thing that Cressida had done when she go back from the funeral was to take Mary Rose upstairs t her bedroom where she had locked her inside, using th newly installed black bolt. Fay Wisherton had bee shocked that Cressida didn't bother to make the chil change her soaked clothing. Mary Rose's teeth were rat ling uncontrollably in her head and her face was blu after her long freezing vigil at the graveside. Fay als found it incomprehensible that Cressida made no effort take a hot drink up to my daughter. Neither did it occur t her that Mary Rose might like something to eat. On Mary Rose was locked in her bedroom, Cressida seeme to feel that all my daughter's needs were satisfied. She' come down to the living room and immediately starte telling Fay Wisherton about the funeral.

'Your wife gave no sign that she had a clue who yo secretary was,' Mrs Butterhorn said. 'Understandab this made the poor girl feel extremely uncomfortabl Your wife didn't seem to have any idea at all why yo secretary had suddenly appeared in her cottage. But s behaved as if she didn't care who Miss Wisherton was where she had come from. She wasn't unfriendly but s gave the impression that she was only glad to see h because she was grateful to have anyone there w could be made to listen to her description of the Sutt funeral.'

'It all sounds very worrying,' I said.

'It's worse than that,' Mrs Butterhorn answered. ' my opinion the situation is becoming really grave.'

My secretary had found it excruciating to be forced hear about Maureen Sutton's burial service. She w mystified as to why my wife had attended it in the fir place for she soon gathered Cressida had never met t Suttons or their child. This burial was an occasion whi by its very nature was bound to be distressing, and it was one that Fay Wisherton would have preferred not to have had described to her. She found it harrowing to be told that the children in Maureen Sutton's school had clubbed together and sent a wreath of lilies to the little murdered girl. Cressida was relentless. She went on talking and talking with frenetic speed. When she spoke about the brass handles on the small brown coffin, tears started streaming down her cheeks.

The worst moment had been when Cressida reached the high-point of her narrative and described Mrs Sutton's agonised reaction when Mary Rose had appeared like a little ghost and thrown the snowdrops into her dead child's grave.

It was then that Fay Wisherton started to find my wife so frightening that if it had not been for her strong sense of loyalty towards myself as her employer – and if she hadn't such a fear that she might be pounced upon by the rapist – she would have taken her suitcase and run for her life towards the Beckham railway station.

'What exactly did my wife do that frightened Fay so much?'

It seemed that although there were tears in her eyes, Cressida had kept smiling her nervous-tic smile as she gave her account of Mrs Sutton's anguished collapse in the graveyard. She had then pressed her finger to her lips as if she was about to divulge an important secret. She had gone up the ladder staircase and when she reappeared, she was accompanied by a livid-faced Mary Rose.

'Mary Rose,' she said. 'Do you remember the lady who was sobbing her eyes out at the funeral – the lady who started howling when we were all standing round the grave?'

Mary Rose had nodded like a little puppet whose head was being jerked by strings.

'Mary Rose . . . do you know why that poor lady was so unhappy?'

Once again my daughter nodded.

'Mary Rose . . . can you tell your Mummy why that lady was howling like a wounded animal?'

'Because her daughter had been raped,' Mary Rose whispered.

'And you haven't forgotten what rape means,' Cressida continued. 'I want you to tell me what that man did to Maureen Sutton when he took her off to the woods. I want you to tell me exactly what he did. I'll be angry if you've forgotten . . .'

It was at this point that Fay Wisherton could bear it no longer and she told my wife she'd left her gloves in Mrs Butterhorn's house. She found it agonising to be present while my daughter was subjected to this unhealthy and brutal inquisition. When my secretary had arrived at Mrs Butterhorn's, she had come in staggering like a drunk and instantly collapsed in tears on the sofa.

'She was as shattered as Tom Crake's sister when she heard her brother had confessed to the killing.'

I asked where Fay Wisherton was at the moment. Apparently she was back with Cressida in the cottage. Mrs Butterhorn had invited my secretary to spend the night. But as she'd promised me that she would keep my wife company she had refused, though she had dreaded returning to the cottage. She was petrified of my wife and found her hateful. She couldn't bear the intense demented expression in Cressida's eyes. When my wife had been talking about the funeral, she had felt she was listening to a woman possessed.

My secretary was finding the cold and the squalor of the cottage extremely disagreeable. But it was the way Cressida was treating Mary Rose that she found insufferable. She'd never seen a mother behave like that to her child. She wondered if I was aware of all the things that were going on.

'And your secretary is right. I don't think you are aware of some of the things your wife is up to. Did you know, for example, that never again is she going to allow your daughter to go to school?'

168

'But that's ridiculous. She has to let Mary Rose go to school.'

'Your wife says it's much too dangerous. She's been told that perverts hang around the playgrounds and that's where they select their victims. She's going to educate Mary Rose herself.'

'But Cressida is barely educated. How can she think she can educate my daughter?'

'Ask her,' Mrs Butterhorn said. 'I don't think she'll change her mind about this. She really seems very firm.'

'Mrs Butterhorn . . . I know what you are saying. You think I've got to act . . . that I've got to act very quickly.'

'Damn right you've got to act!' Mrs Butterhorn's voice acquired the bossy booming tone that I disliked. 'You can't leave your poor secretary in that cottage while you enjoy yourself in London. It really isn't fair on her. You are exploiting her good nature. Why should that poor girl be shut up alone with your wife? Your secretary isn't married to her.'

I agreed that I obviously couldn't expect Fay Wisherton to remain for very long in the cottage. I still didn't know what to do. If I went to a lawyer and started divorce proceedings it would all take time. Meanwhile Cressida's behaviour seemed to be getting more and more worrying by the day.

Mrs Butterhorn said she'd never thought divorce proceedings were the immediate answer. God knows how long they would take. In her opinion Mary Rose shouldn't be left with my wife another day. The child wasn't getting any schooling. She was shut up like a prisoner in her bedroom. The only time she'd been let out recently was when Cressida took her to the funeral. All day long my wife did nothing but talk to her about the dangers of rape. It was incredibly unwholesome.

Mrs Butterhorn's advice to me was to get Mary Rose out of that cottage as soon as possible. I must spirit her away and place her where my wife was unable to find her. I could get the child a nurse. There were many possibilities. The urgent thing was to get her out of the cottage. After that I could consult a lawyer and find out the best thing to do.

I told her I couldn't kidnap Mary Rose tonight. I suddenly felt exhausted. However, I promised I would come down to Beckham the following day and once I'd found out exactly what was going on I'd decide what I ought to do.

'You are really very like Mervyn,' Mrs Butterhorn said insultingly. 'It's hard to make you take positive action. I imagine you both had the same sort of background with lots of nannies and after that all the swank of public school and university. I've rather turned against all that kind of hothouse upbringing lately. It prevents people from maturing. It makes it hard for them to behave like men.'

We said goodbye a little coldly. I resented her parlour analysis and I felt she was urging me into a course of action which might not in the end be to the advantage of myself or my wife or Mary Rose.

Chapter Fifteen

I still felt resentful as I drove down to Kent the following day. I would have much preferred to have stayed in London and worked. Mrs Butterhorn's idea that I ought to abduct Mary Rose from the cottage seemed more and more wild and unfeasible.

When I got to Beckham I decided to go to the Red Lion to have a drink before going to the dreaded cottage. The landlord was behind the bar. He said there had been a nasty scene in the village that morning. Had I heard about it?

I asked him to tell me what had happened. Apparently the police had picked up an eighteen-year-old boy and taken him in a van down to the police station for questioning. The news had spread round the village and a great crowd of women rushed off immediately to the station. When the van arrived they surrounded it and tried to overturn it. 'They went beserk,' he said. 'I heard all this screaming and I went to see what was going on. It was a very nasty sight. You couldn't believe the viciousness of these women once they got together. They were yelling all sorts of obscene things.'

'What kind of things?'

'Well, they were yelling all the things they wanted to do to the boy. They wanted to spike his eyes out, cut off his genitals and stuff them in his mouth - all that kind of unpleasant stuff. Mass female fury is a very frightening thing to see, Sir. I've been in the Army so I've seen a lot. But I didn't like the ugly mood these women were in. You

171

knew that if they managed to overturn that van and get at that boy they were going to do all the things they said they wanted to do to him.'

'But they didn't overturn the van.'

'No, they didn't. But only because the police called in reinforcements. The police were in quite a spot. You had to feel sorry for them. They obviously didn't know how to deal with the situation. They couldn't exactly bash these women on the head. And when they finally broke up the crowd the women turned on them, spitting and hissing and calling them all sorts of obscene names.'

'But who were all these women?'

'They were just nice respectable women from Beckham, Sir. That's what made the whole thing really shocking. I saw the Beckham postmistress in the crowd, and several teachers from our school. Then Mrs Butterhorn was there just yelling her head off. And your wife was there with your little girl . . .'

'Mrs Butterhorn wasn't there!'

'Oh yes, I'm afraid she was, Sir. She was one of the most loud-mouthed and bloodthirsty. She seemed to feel very strongly. And she's a vociferous lady at the best of times, as you probably know.'

'And my wife was there with my little girl?'

'Yes, I'm afraid she certainly was. I must say I didn't think she should have brought a child to that kind of nasty demonstration. Your little girl looked fit to die of fright in a crowd of screaming women all prepared for murder. And your wife didn't look herself, if you don't mind me saying so. Normally she's such a retiring sort of person, but she was shaking her fists and jumping up and down and she was egging the other women on . . .'

'What happened to the boy in the end?'

'Once the police finally dispersed the women they got him safely into the station. They questioned him and they seemed satisfied he was innocent for they very soon released him.'

'So if they'd had their way these women would have

ripped that unfortunate boy to bits and castrated him without bothering to find out if he was guilty?'

'I'm afraid they would, Sir. That's why I found the whole episode very troubling. These were not uneducated hooligan type women from the council estate, you understand. As I said before these were all nice respectable ladies from Beckham itself. And a lot of them have sons themselves. How would they like to have their eighteen-year-old boy blinded and dismembered before he'd ever had the chance of a trial?'

'Oh God,' I said. 'How depressing it all is.'

'It certainly was depressing. That's a very good word to describe it. I work here in this bar and I see a lot that goes on in this village. I'm afraid the killing of that little Sutton girl has had a very bad effect on our community . . .'

After I left the Red Lion I seriously considered driving straight back to London. Not only did I dread the idea of seeing Cressida, but I now dreaded seeing my confidante, my mentor, my conscience, Mrs Butterhorn, having just heard she'd been so bloodthirsty outside the police station. I then realised it would be caddish and despicable to leave Beckham without seeing how Fay Wisherton was faring in the cottage.

She opened the door when I rang. She appeared intensely relieved to see me. It was too obvious that she was extremely unhappy. I had the impression that since she'd been with Cressida, everything about her had turned a paler shade of beige.

Cressida was out. She hadn't told my secretary where she was going. She had gone off dressed in full mourning and wearing her veil, accompanied by darkly clad Mary Rose.

'Where on earth could she have gone to?' I asked Fay. The news that Cressida had gone out filled me with apprehension. Whatever reason she had for leaving the cottage, I knew it was unlikely to be one of which I would approve.

Fay Wisherton said she had no idea where my wife was

or when she planned to return. She only knew she would have felt happier if Cressida hadn't taken Mary Rose.

'I gather from Mrs Butterhorn that you've had a difficult time with my wife.'

Fay Wisherton hesitated. Her natural reticence and delicacy made it difficult for her to be frank with me. She seemed to be on the verge of tears.

'I don't know if I can take much more!' Her voice quavered. 'I hate to let you down but I really don't think I can spend another night in this cottage!'

'I'm sorry'.

Fay Wisherton, seeing my expression of despair, quickly explained that Cressida had been perfectly civil to her. Personally my wife had treated her quite well. That was not the problem.

'It's the way she treats Mary Rose.'

Fay Wisherton started to cry. Her embarrassment at her own display of emotion made it all the more embarrassing for me.

'Would you like a cup of tea? Have a cup of tea,' I kept stupidly repeating.

I took her to the kitchen, which seemed tidier than when I'd last seen it. I realised that my secretary must have cleaned it up. I frantically searched for a tea-bag but failed to find one.

'Don't worry,' she said. 'I don't need tea. Please give me a few minutes. I'll soon pull myself together.'

She said she was exhausted. Cressida had asked her to keep awake for several hours while she herself got some sleep, and then she had come to the guest room and offered to take over the role of sentry, but my secretary felt by that time so wakeful and she was in such a state of angst that she was unable to take advantage of the opportunity to get some rest.

'Your wife moves round the cottage all night long. One hears her creaking along the landing and she goes up and down that staircase. She keeps peering out of the windows into the darkness. Over and over again she kept coming to

174

my door to ask me if I could hear anything. She worked me up to a point that I often thought I could . . .'

I asked my secretary how Cressida had seemed to her that morning. She shrugged impatiently as if she had found the question idiotic.

'You must understand that she is nervously ill at the moment. She wasn't always in the peculiar frame of mind she is in now.'

Once again my secretary shrugged her shoulders.

'Well, I suppose you must have had a good reason for marrying such a person,' she said.

Fay Wisherton had never once before said a critical word to me. The sharpness of this remark was a shock. I felt I'd stepped with bare feet on a drawing pin.

'I did have a good reason,' I said.

My secretary didn't answer. She had quickly reverted and become her usual reticent self. Her innate tact prevented her from trying to make me tell her any more.

'I'll tell you my reason.'

I wouldn't stop. As she tried to retreat and take refuge behind her usual formality, I charged her like a lumbering bull. 'I'll tell you my reason for marrying her. I married her because she was pregnant – because she was having Mary Rose!'

Fay Wisherton and I were not together at midnight when alcohol has burned away the boundaries of good taste and secrets flow with the wine and spill freely on the floor. We were together on a cold, grey English morning in Cressida's desolate kitchen. Not only did we have no wine, neither of us even had a tea-bag. The bars my wife had put on all the windows made us feel like prisoners locked within the cell of our mutual embarrassment.

'What time do you want to go back to London?' I asked her. I had to say something to break the silence.

'I'm afraid you feel I've let you down . . . I hate to disappoint anybody. I can stay here a few more hours if you'd like me to. But I can't quite see what use my presence will be.'

175

'Just tell me what time you want to go. I'll drive you to the station.' I was being noble. By my display of nobility I hoped to make her feel how much I was suffering from her betrayal.

'Are you going to spend the night here?' she asked me hesitantly.

'I'll have to spend the night here. I have no choice since you are going back to London. You must have seen for yourself that my wife is in no state to be left with my daughter on her own.'

'But your wife might as well be left on her own. That's what makes it all so frightful. That's why I want to go back to London!'

'How do you mean?'

Fay Wisherton suddenly became violently emotional and her normally beige cheeks flushed and turned to a sunset pink.

'You could have someone sitting for eternity in this cottage!' she said. 'And they wouldn't be able to prevent your wife from doing exactly what she wants to do.'

'How do you mean?' I knew perfectly well what she meant but I was curious to hear how she would express it.

'She can't leave your little daughter alone. She goes on and on at the child. She was doing it half the night and I was just sitting here and there was nothing I could to stop her. I've never felt so powerless. After all, I'm a stranger to the woman. I had no right to interfere.'

I asked my secretary what my wife had been saying to Mary Rose. It seemed that yesterday the police had given out a warning that Maureen Sutton's killer might well be a married man, that he might have several children of his own. This announcement had apparently ignited Cressida's smouldering fears and fantasies and she had been unable to get it out of her mind.

'She wouldn't stop telling poor little Mary Rose what the police had said. She kept asking her if she knew what it meant. And the poor child was looking fragile as a feather as if any gust of wind could blow her away.'

'I'm afraid my wife thinks she's doing it all for the good of the child,' I said helplessly.

'For the good of the child! My foot!' Anger now streaked my secretary's sunset complexion until it was transfused with veins of red. 'You couldn't believe how your wife carried on. It was a dreadful thing to hear her. She kept warning Mary Rose that she mustn't trust the fathers of any of the children at her school. Even if they seemed friendly, even if she knew them quite well, she must never forget that they could easily be the killer. And then she went into the most ghastly description of what they might do to Mary Rose before they killed her. And she described it all in the crudest of language. She was repulsive. She used anatomical expressions so shocking and dirty, I could never repeat them to you. She realised I was appalled to hear a mother using such vile language to a child. To excuse herself she told me that she didn't want to make sex seem pretty to Mary Rose. She wanted her to realise how filthy and dangerous it was . . .'

I said nothing. Once again the bars on the kitchen windows turned it into a cell and feeling imprisoned together we squirmed with mutual embarrassment. Fay Wisherton had shocked me and she knew it. Hearing what my wife had said to Mary Rose I was frightened by the way her entire personality appeared to have changed. She seemed to have abandoned all the self-made rules that she once had lived by. I remembered that on one occasion I'd said 'damn' when I burnt my hand on the stove. She had instantly reprimanded me with gentleness and courtesy, for that was in the old days. She'd begged me never again to use strong language in front of Mary Rose.

'I hear my wife went off to the police station this morning,' I said. 'It seems that the police picked up a boy for questioning and a lot of the women in Beckham got very excited.'

'Oh yes, your wife certainly went rushing off to the police station.' Fay Wisherton gave a little shudder of disgust. 'She worked herself into a frenzy. It was a horrible sight to see.. She kept telling Mary Rose what she wanted to do to the boy. They were cruel, disgusting things. I would have liked to have blocked your poor little daughter's ears . . .'

I asked how my wife had behaved when she returned. Apparently she'd come back in a sour disgruntled mood.

'She was really quite irrational,' my secretary said. 'She kept muttering rude things about the police. She claimed that even if the boy was guilty the police would still release him. She said males always liked to protect other males . . .'

'Mrs Butterhorn thinks I ought to take Mary Rose away from my wife. Do you think she is right?' I asked.

'Of course she's right!' Fay Wisherton seemed angered by the stupidity of my question.

'You can see that my wife would fight to the death to stop me taking the child. The only way I could get Mary Rose out of this cottage would be to kidnap her bodily. You don't find that rather extreme?'

'This is an extreme situation,' Fay Wisherton said. 'I think you should treat it as such and act accordingly.'

I told her that I was going next door to discuss the whole thing with Mrs Butterhorn. Although I was still smarting from her accusation that I found it difficult to be manly, I still felt that if I were to seize Mary Rose by brute force, the enterprise should be planned with great care, and I needed her advice.

My secretary said she was going upstairs to take a rest. She felt a wreck. She needed to lie down for a while and then she would take the train back to London.

When I went over to Mrs Butterhorn's, Eliza Crake was there sitting on the living room sofa. When I came in, the old woman got up and went shuffling off in a curiously guilty way, as if I'd surprised her doing something illicit.

'That poor woman,' Mrs Butterhorn said when she had gone. 'She can't get over old Tom's confession. She keeps asking me over and over again why I think he confessed.'

'I can understand she might be troubled by that.'

178

'She thinks of nothing else. She says that if he'd turned out to be the real killer, she could hardly feel more ashamed of him.'

'You told me that Eliza Crake has a neurasthenic nature. I imagine that with her highly strung temperament she must be giving the old fellow quite a bad time.'

'Poor old Tom Crake is having the most rotten time. Apparently she berates him day and night. She's cooked for him all his life and now she refuses to do it any more and the wretched old chap has never learnt to turn on a kettle.'

'But that's awful,' I said.

'It certainly is hard on him. But I have to admit I see his sister's point. Why did he confess to the killing? It was a highly peculiar thing for him to do!'

'People do confess to things they haven't done. Tom Crake is certainly not the first.'

'But why do they confess?' Mrs Butterhorn asked. She stared at me belligerently.

'I'm not exactly sure. There are complicated psychological reasons . . .' I could have explained in greater depth but somehow I didn't want to.

I sensed that Mrs Butterhorn was in a man-hating mood. Earlier she had been with all those crazed Beckham women outside the police station. She had been the most vociferous and cried the loudest for blood. I feared that if I were too explicit on this subject she would seize my explanation and somehow manage to turn it against me.

'Do women ever do any of this false confessing?' she asked.

'I've no idea.' This was quite true. I really didn't know. But I had the awful suspicion it might be a phenomenon that was more common among men.

'Is it only sex crimes that all these men confess to? Do they confess to thefts, to bank robberies, to forging cheques and things like that?'

'Mrs Butterhorn . . .' I said frantically. 'I wish you

wouldn't ask me all these questions. I'm a historian. I'm not a criminologist.'

'I quite understand why Eliza Crake doesn't want to cook another sausage for her brother.' Mrs Butterhorn tossed her grey cropped head with such a hostile gesture it was as if she hoped her remark would annihilate me.

This was a mine-strewn conversation and I tried to steer her away from it. I told her that things were getting worse and worse in the cottage.

'What made you think they were likely to improve?'

'I was foolish. I suppose I'm an optimist.'

'You are not an optimist. You are just like Mervyn . . . you only feel happy when your head is in the sand.'

'There's something wrong with your comparison,' I said. 'I'm not trying to hide from anyone.'

'If your head is buried in the sand,' she continued stubbornly, 'you can't see the things that have to be done.'

'Mrs Butterhorn . . .' I protested. 'Please don't get so impatient with me. It's quite clear to me what should be done. Mary Rose must be got out of the cottage. But how can I accomplish that without my wife noticing? It's really not that simple. Even when my daughter is locked in her room, Cressida goes to check that she is alive about every five minutes. I can't get into a situation in which we use Mary Rose like the rope in a tug-of-war.'

Mrs Butterhorn agreed that would be frightening for the child and extremely inadvisable. She still felt there were many ways to surmount the problem. She herself would be quite willing to act as a decoy . . .

She abruptly interrupted herself in order to ask me if I knew that there was a man trying to get into my cottage. This startling information made my heart pound furiously. Suspicion and fear had become like the air one breathed in this detestable village.

I went to a window and I saw there was a man standing at the door of the cottage. I rushed out of Mrs Butterhorn's house and bristling like a guard-dog I asked him quite rudely what he wanted.

180

He was a young man with a narrow unhappy face. He was very neatly dressed in a dark suit and a dark tie. He had fair hair that was slicked down and browned by some kind of hair oil.

He asked me if I was Cressida's husband. When I told him that I was, he asked if he could speak to me privately. I invited him into the cottage. I had to ring the bell because Cressida did not trust me to have a key. Fay Wisherton let us in, having examined us apprehensively for a long time through the spyhole. She was wearing a kimono of some neutral colour. She looked tousled and unwell.

Once the young man and I were inside, my secretary discreetly left us and went back up the ladder staircase to the guest room.

'You want to speak to me?' I asked him.

'I'm afraid I do. I want to talk to you about something extremely embarrassing. I want to talk to you about your wife.'

'I don't think you told me your name. I hope you don't mind me asking you who you are?'

'My name is Sutton,' he replied. 'I'm George Sutton.'

'Oh no! You are not *the* Sutton, not the Sutton that has just had this awful tragedy?'

He nodded speechlessly. I too was dumbfounded. I saw his eyes turn towards the mantelpiece and I felt mortified. What could be more shameful than having a framed photograph of his daughter on my mantelpiece? I couldn't take it down. It was too late; I knew he'd seen it.

'I'd like to say how desperately sorry I am,' I stuttered. I was not only speaking of the murder of his child, I was also referring to the tasteless presence of her photograph. 'There's nothing much one can say,' I continued in desperation.

He shook his head. He was still speechless.

'You wanted to talk to me?'

He nodded. When he finally spoke, his voice was very low and sad. Once again he warned me that the reason for his visit was embarrassing.

'I think you said you wanted to talk to me about my wife.'

'That's what I want to talk to you about. I hate to say this because I know she is trying to be kind. But can I beg you to stop her from coming round to our house?'

'When did she come round?' I felt shattered. This was even worse than the photograph.

Apparently she'd come round that day. She arrived without warning and rang their bell. She brought a little girl with her carrying a big bunch of flowers. Mrs Sutton had told Cressida she was feeling very ill – that she was not in a fit state to see anyone. Cressida had ignored this and claimed she knew how to comfort her. She had pushed past the poor woman and entered the house.

'I can't bear to hear this,' I said. 'It's one of the most upsetting things I've ever heard.'

'I think she meant well,' Mr Sutton said. 'But I think my wife will end up in hospital if she ever does it again.'

'Is she planning to come round to see you again?'

'Oh, indeed she is. She promised she'll be coming back with the little girl tomorrow morning.'

'I'll prevent her,' I said. 'One way or another I swear I'll prevent her from coming round tomorrow!'

'I'd be very grateful if you could do that. I can't tell you how much she upset my wife today. And my wife's been through hell. Both of us have been through hell. We just can't take any more of her visits. We really can't take it!'

'No one could take it,' I said. 'I am so shocked by the whole thing I hardly know how to apologise to you.'

I longed to be able to offer this unfortunate young man a drink. But there was nothing to drink in the cottage. I couldn't even offer him a cup of tea.

'I suppose your wife found out our address from the local directory,' he continued in his low sad voice. 'I'm afraid this ghastly business had made us quite well known.'

182

'All the publicity must be unbearable. But where is my wife at this very moment? For God's sake don't tell me she is still at your house tormenting Mrs Sutton.'

He shook his head. Once again some strong emotion seemed to make him speechless. Finally he said Cressida had left his house about an hour ago. After she left Mrs Sutton had gone into a bout of hysterical grief the like of which he never wished to see again.

'It was all the things that your wife said to Mrs Sutton that did her in. Your wife claimed she was the only person in the world who really understood what we were going through. She said we never left her mind and I believed her.'

'It was perfectly true what she said. But that doesn't make things better.'

'It didn't make things better. Your wife was really very cruel to us. But I don't think she realised it. She reconstructed the whole crime and made us both relive it. I thought Mrs Sutton was going to faint when your wife told her she'd been up to the woods to the place where it happened. She kept talking about the blood in this nervous excited way and Mrs Sutton and I were sitting there listening to her and she couldn't have hurt us more if she'd put a knife right through our hearts.'

'My wife really is insane to have done this to you!'

Once again I had the feeling that my windpipe was choked with red-hot coals.

'She struck us as a very ruthless character,' Mr Sutton said. 'That's why I beg you never to let her come back. She kept telling us all the awful things she wanted to do to the man who murdered our little Maureen. She thought it would cheer us up but it made us feel worse and worse. Mrs Sutton and I take a Christian attitude. We feel that the man who killed Maureen was mentally ill. He'd have to be gravely ill to do a wicked thing like that. That man needs help, he doesn't need punishment.'

'You are very forgiving, Mr Sutton. I am deeply ashamed of the way my wife behaved.'

183

'You know that yesterday she came to my child's burial service?'

'I'm afraid I know that all too well. I promise you, Mr Sutton, I did everything in my power to stop her doing that.'

'I don't know what you did to stop her,' he said bitterly. 'But I know it wasn't successful. There she was in the cemetery . . .'

Mr Sutton got up to leave and I was glad that he was going. I felt inept, confronted by this stricken man who had just suffered such an agonising personal tragedy.

As he was leaving, I suddenly wondered where Cressida could be. 'Mr Sutton, you say my wife left your house an hour ago. I can't understand why she hasn't come home.'

A peculiar tortured look came over his thin face. 'I know where she is. And quite frankly I don't like it at all. She said she was going off to Maureen's grave to pray for her soul. I can't tell you what that did to my wife. That was the thing she minded most of all. We both feel very emotional about that grave. Maureen was our child and we feel her grave is ours. We don't want a strange woman hanging round it. Can you understand that?'

'I certainly can. I'll try to persuade my wife never to go there again.'

The situation was so awful I felt like screaming. I would never forgive Cressida for putting me in this excruciating position with Mr Sutton. After he had gone I thought of going over to Mrs Butterhorn to tell her what Cressida had done to the unlucky Suttons. But I decided the whole thing was too painful. I wanted to forget it – to pretend none of it had happened. I wanted to do what Mervyn Butterhorn had apparently liked to do. I just wanted to bury my head in the sand.

Chapter Sixteen

Cressida didn't return for a long time that evening. When she finally came through the door with Mary Rose, I was enraged by the sight of their funeral outfits. It was horrifying to think that they'd both gone to the house of the Suttons dressed like that. It was an insult, a mockery.

'I went and visited the Suttons today,' said Cressida in the smug exalted tone she had recently acquired.

'Can't you remove that ridiculous black veil if you want to talk to me?' I felt my anger rising.

She did remove it, but most unwillingly.

'I think the Suttons were extremely glad to see us. I think it was an immense comfort to them to know how much we cared.'

She is incredible, I thought. Has there ever been a woman so insensitive?

'I am going back to see them tomorrow. I don't think they should be alone at a time like this. I think it must be a relief to them to know their grief is shared.'

It was then that my rage exploded. I cursed my wife and I called her many ugly violent names. I lost control to a point where I could easily have wrecked the whole cottage. I went crashing over to the mantelpiece and picked up the framed photograph of little Maureen Sutton. I did what I'd wanted to do for a long time. I hurled it in the fire.

Cressida gave a scream when she saw me do this. I wanted revenge for so many things she'd done that I cursed the dead Sutton child because I knew this would seem blasphemous to Cressida and I hoped it would strike her to the heart.

Hearing the shouting and the cursing and the commotion, my secretary came rushing to the top of the staircase in her kimono.

Mary Rose was clinging desperately to her mother's skirts like the survivor of a shipwreck clinging to a raft. I was much too enraged to care if she found the violence of my outburst terrifying. Later I wished I hadn't burnt the photograph in front of her. Later I wished she hadn't heard the spite and the viciousness with which I cursed the murdered child. But at the time it was as if I was trying to exorcise the ghost girl who now haunted the cottage, this little grey spectre who dominated all the life within the household and made it seem like a dwelling that was only fit to be inhabited by the dead.

Cressida just stood there staring at me. The pupils of her eyes had totally vanished. Her face was twisted. It had a terrible expression of venomous hate. If she had had a knife at that moment, I'm certain she would have stabbed me.

If my wife and I quarrelled, we could only do so to our own peril. We'd recognised that in the past when we had been incessantly polite. There was no sexual attraction, no respect or mutual fondness to help heal the bleeding gashes that were bound to result if we pulled down our white truce flag of superficial courtesy.

Seeing the murderous look in Cressida's glassy turquoise eyes, I knew that I must get out of the cottage. If I lingered there a moment more, there could only be some form of catastrophe. I made a dash for the door as if something diabolical was chasing me. I jumped into my car and set off at top speed for London.

After driving crazily for a while, I finally started to cool down a little. Once my mind no longer boiled and churned with vengeful fantasies I wondered what repercussions the scene I'd created in the cottage would have on my wife and daughter. I also started to worry about my secretary. There had been immense callousness in the way I'd abandoned her. I'd left her marooned with my insensate wife in the cottage. But much as I pitied Fay Wisherton's undesirable situation, I knew that nothing would induce me to return to her rescue. I would only ever go back to my wife's benighted dream house in order to kidnap Mary Rose and remove her from the poisonous swamp of her present environment. Fay Wisherton could always escape from my wife and get on a train for London. She had no fetters to keep her imprisoned in the cottage. I said all of this to myself in order to assuage any uncomfortable feelings of conscience. For deep down I suspected that with her honourable and benevolent nature, my secretary would feel it was wrong to leave a child alone with a woman who progressively seemed to be losing touch with reality.

Chapter Seventeen

When I got back to my flat, the first thing I did was to go and collect my secretary's cat from the caretaker of the building. The cat seemed fine; if possible she looked even more overfed and sybaritic than when I'd last seen her. It then occurred to me that I'd never bothered to tell poor Fay Wisherton that I'd left her beloved animal in responsible hands. Her anxiety at finding herself locked away in exile with a woman as unsettling as Cressida was probably being intensified by the fact that every moment she served the wicked sentence I'd imposed upon her, she was worrying ceaselessly about her cat.

It struck me that it would be decent, what Mrs Butterhorn would call 'manly', if I were to ring my secretary to tell her the animal was perfectly all right. Unfortunately at that point my nerve failed me, just as Mrs Butterhorn no doubt could have predicted it would. Cressida might answer the telephone and I couldn't bear to speak to her. Although I'd said many violent and injurious things to my wife that day, there were still many festering resentments which I'd not yet expressed.

Cressida had been taken by surprise by my tornado-like outburst. I'd showered her with curses. I'd burnt the effigy of Maureen Sutton. I'd then cursed the violated child. My performance had been uniquely discreditable. Yet Cressida had done nothing in retaliation. She had just glared at me with pupilless eyes. But by now she would have had the time to brood on all the things I'd done and muster the forces of her own fury. I couldn't bear to speak to her even if I was torturing Fay Wisherton by refusing to give her reassuring news of her cat.

Lacking the courage to ring the cottage, I instead telephoned Mrs Butterhorn. I told her she was wrong to say I lacked the ability to take any positive action. Tomorrow I was planning to abduct Mary Rose from under her mother's roof. I didn't know what the consequences would be, but I'd worry about that later.

'So you are really going to do it,' she said. 'Good for you. I didn't think you had it in you.'

Ignoring her little insult I asked her how she thought the whole thing would best be accomplished.

She said she would be more than willing to act as a decoy. She had a stratagem. She would ring up Cressida and try and lure her away from the cottage. She would imply that she had vital information as to the identity of the Beckham rapist. It was unlikely that Cressida, with her frenetic interest in the recent killing, would be able to resist such enticement. There was only one danger. She might bring Mary Rose, in which case, the whole plan would fail and we would have to devise another scheme.

I told Mrs Butterhorn I thought her stratagem a clever one. If Fay Wisherton was in the cottage, Cressida would be much more likely to go to Mrs Butterhorn's without the child. I couldn't imagine any circumstances under which Cressida would leave Mary Rose if there was no one else in the house. There was another reason why it was vital that my secretary should be there at the time of the kidnapping. If Cressida were to go next door as we both hoped, I needed someone to let me in so that I could rush upstairs and seize the child in her mother's absence.

As we hatched the plot, I became increasingly terrified that my secretary would find it intolerable in the cottage and that she would take a train back to London as she had said she was going to do. I was hoping that she would be too conscientious to leave Mary Rose alone with a woman who was in the frenzied state that Cressida must surely be in after having seen me burn Maureen Sutton's photograph. But I couldn't rely on Fay Wisherton being so altruistic. She was human. She had told me she was going back to London. I'd rushed out of the cottage, cursing and shouting, and driven off to London without saying a word to her. She might well feel aggrieved by my behaviour and decide that if anything unfortunate was to happen to Mary Rose, it was entirely my fault and not in any way her affair.

I therefore asked Mrs Butterhorn if she could use some pretext to speak to Fay Wisherton without Cressida knowing. Could she implore her on my behalf to stay one more night in the cottage so she could be there tomorrow to assist us with the attempted kidnapping? Mrs Butterhorn promised to do this and we agreed to talk in the morning and decide on the exact time the abduction should take place.

I felt curiously relieved after this conversation. The plan had been made and now all I had to do was carry it out. I no longer dithered. I had ceased to be plagued by cowardly hesitations and considerations. Feeling quite excited by the prospect of the next day's enterprise, I drank some whisky and looked through my notes on Hertha Ayrton.

Just as I was about to go to sleep, my telephone rang. To my astonishment it was Gloria. By now I'd adjusted to the idea that I'd never hear from her again. The turmoil of my recent experiences in Beckham had not cured the wound that had been left by her rejection. But it had prevented me from having the emotional time to explore it.

'Rowan . . .' she said. She sounded nervous. 'I just want to make it clear that I'm not telephoning you for any personal reasons. I haven't reconsidered my decision. That remains the same . . .'

'How nice of you to tell me that,' I said sarcastically. 'So why are you ringing me?'

'I thought you ought to know that I've been having the most desperate telephone calls from Fay Wisherton.'

'From Fay Wisherton!' I was mystified as to why my secretary had rung Gloria. They knew each other only very slightly. Gloria quite liked Fay, although she made fun of her and said she had a beige heart which was overflowing with beige love for me. But if anything was wrong in the cottage, I couldn't see why my secretary hadn't contacted me directly. I saw no reason why she should have involved Gloria.

Apparently something dreadful had happened but Fay couldn't bring herself to tell me what it was. Yet it was something she found so alarming that she felt she simply had to confide in someone who was fond of me.

'For God's sake, tell me what has happened!'

Gloria said she too had been puzzled when she first received Fay Wisherton's call. She couldn't understand what on earth my secretary could be doing down in the cottage with my wife.

I said that was a long story and one that I'd explain later. Could she please tell me what Fay Wisherton was alarmed about?'

'It was all rather garbled and difficult for me to follow. I understand you had a row with your wife and you burnt a photograph of the poor little girl who got murdered.'

'I know that makes me sound awful. I promise I had a good reason to do it.'

'I don't know your reason. I must say it doesn't sound a very attractive way to carry on.'

'Please, Gloria . . . I don't feel this is the moment for a lecture. Could you just go on with the story?'

'Understandably your wife was very shocked when you destroyed the photograph. After you'd rushed off, she sat on the sofa and wouldn't speak for quite a while. Then a funny knowing look came into her eyes and she told Fay she thought she knew why you had burnt it. Her behaviour became increasingly odd and she kept roaming restlessly around the cottage. At one moment she was laughing hysterically and the next tears were streaming down her cheeks. She kept muttering to herself like a woman talking in her sleep.'

'Could Fay make out anything she was saying?'

'Apparently most of it sounded like gibberish. Only one sentence was clear and she kept repeating it over and over again.'

'What was the sentence?'

'It all falls into place . . . now I can see, it all falls into place.'

'Cressida seems to have gone round the bend lately. So there's not much point in our trying to work out what she meant. It could mean anything.'

'Certainly Fay thinks your wife is a deeply disturbed woman. And her behaviour has become much more frightening since you had the row with her. You seem to have done something to her which has pushed her right over the top. But then you've always liked to give the leaning tree a shove. You have a gift for doing that,' Gloria said aggressively.

'Please, Gloria . . . Could we avoid any personal jibes? Obviously it was a mistake to create the scene I did. But I want to know what Fay thinks I should do now.'

'She thinks you should try and rescue your daughter from that cottage tonight.'

'Oh God, so it has got as bad as that?'

'Your secretary thinks it has,' said Gloria.

I asked her if she knew how Cressida was treating Mary Rose. At some point that evening, apparently, my wife had got her out of bed. She had brought her down to the living room and put her on her knee and held her as if she was an infant. She had then started giving her a lot of warnings. She must never take sweets from strangers. She must never accept a lift in any man's car. She reminded her that Maureen Sutton had got into a man's car. If she hadn't been so trusting, she would still be alive. Then Cressida had started crying, rocking Mary Rose backwards and forwards. 'Poor baby,' she said, 'poor baby, it's so hard to protect you.' It was at that point that my secretary heard her say something so wicked that she could only tell it to Gloria. She couldn't bring herself to tell me personally.

'What did she say?'

'She told your daughter she must never trust any man at all. "They can all be bloody killers," she hissed at the child. "Even your own father." '

'But that's really insane! Surely Cressida can't think that I . . .'

'I'm afraid she does suspect that you did it. Fay is terrified that in the malevolent crazy mood your wife is in, she may try to do you a lot of harm.'

'What kind of harm?' I asked.

Evidently Cressida had at one moment gone up to Fay. Her eyes were glazed. She looked like a woman in a trance. She told Fay that the police had announced on the radio that it was the duty of all the residents of Beckham to report anything they found suspicious. Cressida had burst into a fit of maniacal laughter. 'I have quite a lot to tell them,' she said.

'Fay thinks there's a nasty possibility she may denounce you to the police. If she does that, it will be ghastly for you. There will be publicity. It will be a nightmare of unpleasantness.'

'But she can't denounce me! It's ridiculous. They'll lock her up. She hasn't got a scrap of evidence against me.'

'I know she hasn't,' said Gloria. 'It's quite clear she's raving mad. If she wasn't so mad she'd remember you didn't leave the cottage the evening the child was murdered. You stayed at home and watched television with Mary Rose.'

My heart sank. I'd forgotten I'd told Gloria that pointless lie. If Cressida were to try and make trouble for me, and if there were police inquiries, the fact I'd lied to anyone about my movements on that vital evening would not look very good.

'The only thing that is stopping her from contacting the police is her anxiety about your daughter's reputation,' Gloria said. 'I don't think she has a grain of love and loyalty in her heart towards you. She would denounce you without the slightest compunction if you were not Mary Rose's father. She is only hesitating now because she can't bear the world to know that her daughter is the child of a rapist and a murderer. She is therefore in a dilemma which is totally barmy and off-beam. But to her it's real. Fay thinks you ought to take it seriously.'

I asked Gloria why Fay felt it was so important that Mary Rose be rescued from the cottage that night. It seemed that Cressida had said some wild things to her. She had appeared to be drunk, although she wasn't drinking, and she suddenly started talking about her life.

'Did you know that your wife is the daughter of a Soho prostitute?' Gloria asked me.

'No!'

'She doesn't know who her own father is, just that he was one of her mother's many clients. She had a horrible childhood. Her bedroom was next to her mother's room. She could hear all sorts of hideous things going on. She used to lie in bed and think of ways to murder her mother's lovers.'

'She never told me about that,' I said.

'She was eventually abandoned by her mother. After that she went to various foster homes. I gather her life was extremely grim. But she always had this dream that she wanted to bring up a little girl in the country.'

'A pretty rotten dream it's turned out to be,' I said bitterly.

'Your wife feels that too. That's why Fay thinks the situation is very dangerous. At one point Cressida said that she realised no one could escape from evil in this world, that it was everywhere. She felt it would be better for Mary Rose if she took her to a place where she could never come to any harm. In that way the child would not have to grow up in the shadow of your disgrace. I think she plans to leave a note for the police in which she will denounce you.'

'How is poor Fay dealing with all this?'

'Fay is beside herself. She's climbing the wall with worry. She is trying to encourage your wife to keep talking, although she hates being made to listen to all her deluded ravings. Fay believes that if your wife were to stop talking, she would do something deeply destructive.'

'I'd better go down there tonight,' I said.

'I think you had better,' Gloria agreed.

'If I succeed in rescuing Mary Rose, could I bring her to your flat? Just for the first night? She will feel frightened and lost without her mother. You would be much better at looking after her than I would.'

Gloria hesitated. It was clear that this idea didn't appeal to her at all. But she admitted that the situation was an exceptional one and finally she agreed, with a certain amount of martyrdom. It would be very late by the time I got back to London with the child. She wasn't going to wait up for me. However, I could ring her bell and wake her.

'You do realise Mary Rose can't move in with me for ever,' she said.

After that I telephoned Mrs Butterhorn and explained there was an emergency. My secretary felt that Cressida was becoming increasingly deranged and she now had the delusion that I was responsible for the death of Maureen Sutton. Fay was terrified that she was planning to kill both herself and Mary Rose and leave a note to the police denouncing me as the killer.

Mrs Butterhorn listened without answering for a while. If there can be such a thing as a thunderstruck silence there was one then.

'I don't think you have to worry about her denunciation,' she finally said. 'There are many things in this grisly situation that you certainly ought to worry about. But you don't have to bother about that.'

'How do you mean?' I asked her quickly.

'You couldn't have killed that child. That's all I mean.'

'Mrs Butterhorn, for God's sake tell me why you are so certain. This is really urgent.'

195

'I know you didn't kill that child because I know exactly where you were during the period when she was abducted.'

'And where was I?'

'You were in my potting shed!'

'In your potting shed?'

'Yes, you were underneath my fuchsia seedlings if you want me to be precise.'

'Underneath your fuchsia seedlings!'

'Yes, you were in a pretty sorry state that evening. I think we can both admit that.'

'I do admit it. That's why it's vital that you tell me anything you know about my movements on that evening. I can't remember anything. Now I hear that Cressida is convinced I did the murder, quite frankly I feel terrified. If the police were to question me I would be unable to give them an alibi.'

'I can supply them with all the necessary answers,' Mrs Butterhorn said. Never had this bossy lady seemed so lovable to me.

As she reconstructed my lost evening, I felt like a condemned prisoner who hears that he has been reprieved. Mrs Butterhorn had gone to the Red Lion about six o'clock. I had arrived about six thirty. I had come through the swing door of the pub, my face dark and scowling. Mrs Butterhorn assumed I had just quarrelled with my wife. I was obviously in a fearful rage. I'd pushed through the other customers in the most ill-mannered and violent fashion. Once I reached the bar I'd immediately started ordering double whiskies in such quick succession that Mrs Butterhorn had wondered if she ought to try to restrain me, for she felt there was a suicidal intention in the way I was drinking. She had decided she didn't know me well enough to beg me to be more moderate. She feared I might see it as gross interference on the part of a stranger.

In the hour and a half that I spent in the Red Lion she calculated that I must have consumed at least two whole bottles of whisky. At a certain point I myself must have realised that I had better stop. I suddenly left the bar and staggered like a stage drunk towards the door.

'I was such a fool,' she said. 'I let you go out through the door and it was only when you had disappeared that I realised I should have given you a lift home. Once it was too late I realised it was a crime to let a man in your condition drive a car. If you were to have some hideous smash-up I knew I'd feel responsible. I rushed after you but once I got outside the pub, I saw that you'd somehow managed to get your car started and you were already off. There's nothing worse than knowing what you should have done once it's too late to do it!'

'That's certainly not the most pleasant feeling,' I said.

Mrs Butterhorn had apparently considered telephoning the police. For my own sake she had felt she ought to get them to stop my car. As my neighbour, however, she had been unwilling to involve me in a charge of drunken driving. She had therefore decided to follow me, praying that I'd get home without some fearful mishap.

'How was my driving that evening?' I asked her nervously.

'It was an abomination, to be frank with you. As I followed your car, my heart was in my mouth. You were zigzagging all over the road. You had some perilous near misses, I'm telling you. Once you'd got safely back to your cottage, I wanted to go down on my knees to thank your guardian angel for having protected you.'

'What time did I get back to the cottage? Can you remember, Mrs Butterhorn? It's of the utmost importance.'

'About eight o'clock.'

'So I couldn't possibly have been in the woods at that time?'

'You certainly weren't in the woods. You were in the woods metaphorically. But not in the sense that you mean.'

Once I'd got home I had apparently got out of my car, stumbling and lurching, and instead of going towards the cottage, I'd starting weaving towards Mrs Butterhorn's house.

'You were drunk as a skunk,' she said. 'You didn't really seem to know where you were. But as I watched you going through my gate, I felt there was something funny going on. Although you could hardly stand up, you seemed to know almost as if by instinct that you didn't want to go home to bed in your cottage. It was as if you didn't care where you went just as long as it was in the opposite direction to your wife.'

Once I'd gone through Mrs Butterhorn's gate, I had apparently swerved to the right and it was then that I had had a bad fall, tripping on the stones of her rock garden and crashing down, cutting my hands and knees. I had passed out and however much she shook me, she couldn't make me respond. I groaned but wouldn't wake.

When she'd realised it was impossible to rouse me, she had wondered if she ought to go and tell Cressida that I was unconscious in her garden and ask her to help carry me back to the cottage. Something had stopped her doing this. She suspected that Cressida and I must have had some kind of marital dispute which had triggered off my bout of frantic drinking. If Cressida and I were at each other's throats, she didn't feel it would be very kind to let my wife see me at an obvious disadvantage. She decided to give me the opportunity to sober up before I returned home. I was a dead-weight that evening and strong as she was, she found it impossible to carry me. She managed, however, to drag me a few yards, and deposited me on the floor of her potting shed under the table that held her boxes of fuchsia seedlings. She covered me with a dog-blanket and started working in her garden as she wanted to keep an eye on me, in case I suddenly woke up.

'It was getting quite dark but I had my oil lamp to work by,' she said. 'You didn't inconvenience me at all. To be honest, I was quite grateful for your presence. It forced me to get round to doing some pricking out that I should have done weeks ago.'

I had evidently remained in my stupor for several hours during which time Mrs Butterhorn had continued peacefully pricking out. Every once in a while she had come into the potting shed to check that I was all right.

Finally she had heard me stirring. When she came in to see me, I was half awake and looked terrified and dazed. I didn't seem to know who she was. I was obviously amazed to find myself in the potting shed. Mrs Butterhorn had managed to get me to my feet and she half carried me towards the cottage. She found my front door key in my wallet and she let me in and deposited me on the sofa in the living room, where I promptly passed out again.

'I don't remember any of this,' I said.

'I'm not surprised,' Mrs Butterhorn answered. 'I've rarely seen a man so drunk.'

'I am extremely glad to know that I was in your potting shed at the time that child was abducted,' I said. 'But I am also highly embarrassed that I caused you so much trouble.'

'We all have our ups and downs,' she said cheerfully. 'Don't give it another thought. All you should think about is your daughter.'

I told her I was going to try to get Mary Rose out of the cottage that night. I thought I could get to Beckham by about twelve thirty. I would ring her from a call-box on my arrival. Could she somehow warn my secretary what I was planning to do, for I wanted her to be ready to let me in if we were to succeed in enticing Cressida out of the cottage.

Mrs Butterhorn said she was worried that my wife might think it very strange if she telephoned her so late at night and asked her to come over to her house on the grounds she had news about the killer. I thought it was worth trying all the same. There was a hope that Cressida was in such an irrational state she wouldn't find it abnormal.

Mrs Butterhorn promised to do everything I'd asked her. 'Good luck and God speed,' she said.

Chapter Eighteen

I got to Beckham about twelve thirty. I rang Mrs Butterhorn from a call-box and asked her if she'd managed to contact my secretary to tell her what was happening. Mrs Butterhorn had gone over to the cottage and pretended one of her dogs was ill. She'd asked Fay as an animal expert to give her some advice. In this way she'd been able to talk to my secretary alone and had quickly told her the plan. Apparently Mary Rose was at that moment locked up in her bedroom. Cressida was crouched on the living room floor in a foetal position, rocking backwards and forwards and crying.

I told Mrs Butterhorn I would park my car some distance away from the cottage so that my wife would not hear it arrive. I would then walk to Mrs Butterhorn's house and hide myself in her garden while she telephoned Cressida.

Five minutes later, I was crouching behind one of Mrs Butterhorn's tool sheds. Through the window of her living room I saw her go to the telephone. She talked to Cressida for quite a while. I had no way of knowing how the conversation was going. Finally Mrs Butterhorn stopped talking.

Then I heard a noise. It was the sound of bars being unlocked in the cottage. I could hardly believe it. I saw my wife coming up the path towards Mrs Butterhorn's front door. I saw her face illuminated for a moment by a door lantern, and I'd certainly never seen her look so terrifying.

She went into Mrs Butterhorn's house and I made a

dash and jumped over the fence that separated the garden from the back yard of the cottage. I knocked on the cottage door and my secretary let me in. I rushed up the ladder staircase and unlocked the bolt on the door of Mary Rose's bedroom.

'It's Daddy,' I said and I picked her up in a blanket. She gave a terrified little whimper. I noticed that above her bed Cressida had stuck up a picture of Maureen Sutton.

I didn't rip it down. At this point I felt it could be left there. If my wife chose to turn the cottage into a shrine dedicated to the murdered child, I had no objection, just as long as Mary Rose no longer lived there.

I carried my daughter down the stairs and out of the door. I then ran about a hundred yards to the place I'd parked my car and pushed her into the front seat, where she slumped without making a sound. I drove off through the narrow cobbled streets of Beckham, not daring to go too fast. I knew there were police about and the last thing I wanted was to be caught speeding.

Once out of Beckham, I drove through the dark country lanes that led to the M2.

Just when I felt I could finally relax, that the whole enterprise had been successful, I heard the scream of police sirens. The noise grew louder. It grew more menacing. I realised that the police were after me. Cressida must have telephoned them and reported that her child had been abducted by the killer.

I should have stopped my car. I should have waited for the police to catch up with me and explained to them that I was the father of Mary Rose, that I was taking my daughter to London in order to get her away from a mother who seemed to be in the grip of an advanced psychosis. I should have asked them to contact Mrs Butterhorn and Fay Wisherton, who would have confirmed my testimony.

I did none of these sensible things. As the police sirens grew louder, my only instinct was to flee. I had in my mind the image of that menacing blue line of men advancing slowly through the woods. They were hunters and I felt the primitive terror of the hunted. Instead of braking, I put my foot on the accelerator. Never was there a more insane thing to do. For then the chase began.

I went speeding through the lanes, my tyres screeching as I ricocheted round corners. I missed several collisions with oncoming cars only by fluke. Behind me the sirens grew louder. There seemed to be more of them. Extra police cars had joined the hunt.

I got on to the M2 and drove flat out. In my mirror I could see behind me the menacing blue rotating lights. I felt exhilarated by the speed at which I was travelling. The headlamps of the cars that passed me going in the other direction merged their blazing gold and formed a solid lane of light.

Beside me Mary Rose sat silent and huddled like a little old woman bundled in her blanket. Everything seemed unreal, the screaming sirens, the blinding lights. I felt as though I was in a movie. I seemed to be losing the police cars. I had a sudden moment of maniac exaltation. I felt I'd escaped not only from those dreaded police cars, but finally from Cressida too. I had stolen Mary Rose away from her. I had stolen the rock with which Cressida had been able to weight me down and keep me trapped in the sack of my dreadful marriage. For the first time since her birth, I felt positive affection towards the child. I was glad she was beside me in the car. When I had seen Mary Rose in the past it had only ever been with Cressida and I could therefore only see her as Cressida's creation. This had prevented me from having any sense of responsibility towards her. Now that I had abducted her, I felt that my whole relationship with Mary Rose was going to change. At last she seemed like my daughter.

The passing headlamps now looked gold with promise. I had a wonderful sense of release. My car seemed to lift its wheels from the tarmac. It was as if we were flying through space. I felt that I was a prince and that I'd freed

Mary Rose from a curse.

And then a sudden blast of cold wind entered the car from the side. For a moment I was so shocked and confused I didn't realise there had been a catastrophe. Then I glanced sideways and saw the door of the car was flying open. I had a feeling of vertigo. I jammed my foot on the brakes. The car went into a skid. I desperately wrenched the wheel, trying to get into control again. My tyres still seemed to be skating as if the road was an ice rink. Then I hit the wall of a bridge with a crash. The car swung round and shuddered, then stopped. I sat there stunned. I had a sharp pain in my head where it had hit the windscreen. My knees also hurt. I looked down and saw they were bleeding. For a moment I couldn't take in what had happened. Then with a sickening sense of horror, I realised. Mary Rose had thrown herself out of my car.

I opened the door and jumped out. Despite my giddiness, I started running frantically back down the highway to where she was lying. She was close to the edge of the road. She didn't move. She had lost her blanket and she was only wearing her nightdress. She looked like a little crumpled white bird. She reminded me of Wendy in *Peter Pan* when the Lost Boys shot her with their arrows. I knelt down beside the child. Her eyes were closed. A trickle of blood was coming out of her mouth. I was certain she was dead.

The police cars had stopped a few yards away. The men had got out of their cars, but oddly enough they didn't move. They just stood there. They'd chased my car thinking they were on the trail of the Beckham rapist. Now they had caught me, I couldn't understand why they didn't come forward and grab me. But it was as if they were so shocked and amazed by the turn of events that they were rooted to the spot.

Various lorries were drawing up. Motorists and cyclists were leaving their vehicles in order to gather round. There was the vulture crowd that always assembles to see the accident.

I put my hand on the puny little chest of Mary Rose. I couldn't believe it. I felt like weeping. Her heart was still beating. I felt overwhelmed with joy and relief.

I went and got her blanket and very gently wrapped her up. When I lifted her, she seemed light as tissue paper. 'Oh my God!' I thought. 'Now I've done something unforgivable. She may have internal injuries. You aren't meant to move the victims of road accidents. How could the police have stood there like clods and let me do it? Have they all lost their heads?' Did they feel like me it was wrong to leave her lying in the road?

I started carrying her to the police. I moved at a funeral creep, terrified I might jolt her. I glanced down at the child and she looked so pale and pitiable I could hardly bear to look at her. For the first time I realised the extent to which she had been damaged. She had preferred to die rather than travel in the same car as her own father. There was no way of telling how great her physical injuries might be. But even if by a miracle they were slight, I could see little cause for rejoicing. She'd been injured in ways no hospital could heal.

As I walked towards the police it was as if I was carrying them Mary Rose like an offering. Seeing the police standing there in such large numbers, I felt they'd been summoned to the scene of a crime. Yet their presence was totally unnecessary. There hadn't been any crime. There had just been a nasty road accident. Ambulance men with a stretcher would have more function in this situation that all those uniformed men with truncheons.

When I looked at the white face of Mary Rose, she still seemed to be unconscious and I was glad of that. Temporarily at least she was at peace. She hadn't been killed like Maureen Sutton, but I felt she had certainly been violated.

Nothing seriously illegal had occurred on this desolate stretch of British highway. There was nothing to keep the police hanging around. They might as well go away with their patrol cars and rotating lights and screaming sirens.

There was no crime for them here. There was only evidence that in the past some kind of crime had been committed. And the only proof of this was the fact that Mary Rose had thrown herself out on the tarmac, that she'd deliberately opened the door of my speeding car. But this was not a matter for the police. It was out of their jurisdiction.

'Is there an ambulance on its way?' I asked a police sergeant. I stood in front of him with Mary Rose dangling in my arms. 'This is my daughter,' I said. 'I don't know if you realise that.'

He coughed nervously as he looked at the unconscious child.

'We gathered that, Sir. We had a telephone call from your wife. She gave us a description of your car. That's why we came on your tail. Your wife said that only you could have abducted her daughter. She said other things too. But we won't go into that right now. The child looks to me as if she's in a critical condition.'

Once again he looked at Mary Rose and I felt the poor little girl was shrivelling under his policeman's gaze.

'I've no doubt that you received an hysterical call from my wife,' I said briskly. 'I don't want to hear about it for the moment. I will explain all that later. At this point I only want to get my daughter to the hospital. Why is the ambulance taking so long?'

'The ambulance is on its way. You don't have to worry about that. It's all under control.'

'Obviously I'm worried. My daughter is very badly injured. What else is there to worry about?'

'I think you may have quite a lot to worry about. I'm afraid we won't be able to let you go, Sir. There are some questions we would like you to answer.'

For the first time I looked him in the face. I saw the accusation in his eyes. I saw the anger. He had dark blue eyes that perfectly reflected the colour of his uniform.

'All my men are family men, Sir,' he said grimly. 'We don't like seeing children getting hurt.'

'But I didn't do anything to her . . .' I heard myself stuttering. I had no composure. I felt I was wriggling like an impaled insect under his contemptuous dark eyes. He interrupted my feeble protests impatiently.

'You kidnapped this child from her mother's house. Am I correct, Sir?'

'But she's my daughter.'

'We don't care whose daughter she is. That doesn't concern us much. The little girl looks as if she's been badly smashed up. And we would like to know how it happened. If that child dies, you may find yourself in a very nasty situation. In our experience, children don't just fall out of cars in the routine course of events. But we shall ask you to explain all that when we take you back for questioning . . .'

'May I get a lawyer?'

'Certainly you may get a lawyer, Sir. But you may find you need more than a lawyer to answer the charges your wife is bringing against you. She claims she has evidence that connects you with the killing of the Sutton child.'

'My wife is insane.'

'Quite frankly, she didn't sound very insane to us. Admittedly she sounded distraught, but now it would seem as if she had very good reason to be upset. She told us that her little daughter had been seized from her bed by a man who was so evil and dangerous that she never again expected to see her child alive . . .'

The police sergeant threw another uneasy glance at the unconscious little figure of Mary Rose. He compressed his lips fiercely and he frowned.

I heard the hubbub and wail of an approaching ambulance. Nothing seemed real. The crowds of onlookers were growing larger. More and more cars kept stopping and their passengers got out to gather round and gape.

A series of disconnected and vivid images flashed like hallucinations through my mind. I saw rows of police scouring a wintry tract of leafless woodland. They had wolves on leashes. The wolves were hungry, I could tell by

206

the way they bayed. I saw Cressida dressed in the full mourning she had worn for the funeral of the Sutton child. She was standing in a witness box. She lifted her heavy black veiling in order to testify. Her beautiful blonde face looked tragic but curiously serene. Nothing in her demeanour suggested she suffered from any emotional imbalance. When she spoke, she was immensely dignified. She delivered her testimony in a low flat tone. She obviously believed every word that she said. She was speaking from the heart and this gave conviction to her indictment. She had a single-minded purpose and this had brought her calm. She asked for nothing but vengeance.

This image of the black-veiled Cressida faded and was replaced by a vision of Mrs Butterhorn. She was also in a witness box. Unfortunately she was wearing her seaman's rubber waders. She boomed at the jury in a mannish upper-class accent and I could see they didn't like her. Never had her grey hair been more badly cut. On one side she had chopped off a great chunk and there was a pink patch where she had made herself bald. Never had Mrs Butterhorn's nails looked so dirty. Never had her desire to flout the conventions been more unwelcome. Never had she seemed so supremely disreputable.

'You'd better be coming along with us,' the police sergeant said. His voice sounded very far away, like the voices one hears as one comes round from an anaesthetic.

Mary Rose was taken from my arms. The police sergeant took me by the elbow and brusquely steered me towards one of his patrol cars.

I looked back at Mary Rose as they gently lifted her inert little form on to a stretcher and put her in the ambulance. If by some miracle she survived this accident, I wondered what her future was going to be. She should never be made to live with Cressida again. But her destiny now seemed to be in the authoritative hands of the police and I doubted if there was much that I would be able to do to control it. And if the child were to survive and even if she were to be removed by law from Cressida's unhealthy custody, I wondered if she would ever manage to escape from the demon-infested murky world of her mother, if for Mary Rose the plunge towards the tarmac would not always seem safer than life.